FIRE:

An Account of the Curious Adventures of the Presleys of Fox Hollow Farm

S EDWARD PARKER

For Phoenix

ISBN: 978-1-48357-451-6 (print)
ISBN: 978-1-48357-452-3 (ebook)

CONTENTS

Chapter 1 - The Discovery   1

Chapter 2 - The Presleys   6

Chapter 3 - Gone   12

Chapter 4 - The Chamber   19

Chapter 5 - The Elements   25

Chapter 6 - Fox Hollow   35

Chapter 7 - Dr. Lovejoy   41

Chapter 8 - The Peabody   45

Chapter 9 - Westville   53

Chapter 10 - Argus Finch   61

Chapter 11 - Historical Society   66

Chapter 12 - Mrs. Goodwyn   72

Chapter 13 - Two Invitations   85

Chapter 14 - The Flame   97

Chapter 15 - The Sermon   105

Chapter 16 - The Playdate   113

Chapter 17 - Maritime Museum   122

Chapter 18 - The Key   130

Chapter 19 – The Hospital   140

Chapter 20 – The Recovery   145

Chapter 21 – The Campout   158

Chapter 22 – The Break In   171

Chapter 23 – The Hospital Again   178

Chapter 24 – Captain McKain   185

Chapter 25 – Flight School   193

Chapter 26 – The Epic Sleepover   198

Chapter 27 – The Choice   208

Chapter 28 – Birthday   219

Chapter 29 – Combustion   224

Chapter 30 – Bears   228

Chapter 31 – Rescue   233

Chapter 32 – The Hero   237

Epilogue   241

CHAPTER 1

The Discovery

"WHAT THA?.." is all he managed to get out of his mouth as the trap door beneath his feet fell away and he began plummeting into the darkness. The swift decent reminded him of flying. He always dreamed of flying, but this was different, of course, it was falling. He could barely make out his surroundings during the split-second decent, but just before he hit the bottom he tensed and seemed to slow down and break his own fall.

"Ummph!!"

Well, maybe not break his fall because that hurt something awful. He landed on his left side and banged his head on the ground. The wind was definitely knocked out of him.

"SAMSON! SAMSON! ARE YOU OK! Oh my God!! He fell! SAMSON!!"

The voices were coming from above and his head was spinning. He could hardly breathe. It was dark but oddly warm.

"Go get Dad!," the voices said, panicked. "SAMSON!!!"

He rolled over on his back and tried to open his eyes. He was blinded by a bright circular light directly over his head penetrating the dust pit he was laying in. After a few moments he was able to catch his breath and survey his body. His shoulder hurt. He slowly moved his arm. It was sore, but didn't seem to be broken. His head was throbbing. He reached up to touch his head. Something wet was getting into his eyes so he wiped his face with his hand.

"OUCH!"

When he pulled his hand away, it was covered with a wet, sticky red liquid. The fall had left a huge gash in his forehead and it was bleeding.

"SAMSON!!! Are you OK? Can you hear me?" The voice was more urgent now and pulled him into the present.

"Yes," he coughed quietly. It was hard to get the words out. His throat was dry. The blood was running down his face and into his mouth now. He spit and turned over on his hands and knees.

"I'm OK," he said louder.

"Oh my god! Are you hurt?" the voice continued.

"I've busted my head but I think I'm ok." he said, gaining his composure.

"Hold on. Wylde went to get Dad. We'll get you out in a minute." It was Castilia, she was taking charge as usual.

His eyes were adjusting to the darkness and he began to survey his surroundings. He was laying in what looked like a domed room. The hole that he fell though was at the center of the dome. It looked like the temple in Paris that he has seen in a movie with the open oculus in the center. He must have fallen about 30 feet and should have been hurt much more than he was. That opening in the ceiling was really high up. He couldn't believe he fell all that way. It was hard to see the whole room but it looked like it was round.

He slowly stood up. The blood rushed to his head and he felt dizzy but managed to steady himself.

He was standing at the center of this large room in a rather large depressed circular pit about 12' wide with a stone edge. That must have been what he hit his head on. The earth under him was dry but mossy, which must have cushioned his fall. He walked out of the pit to find more sturdy ground. The floor seemed to be carved out of solid bedrock.

"I'm in some sort of tomb, I think. It looks like there are paintings on the walls. Some sort of cave paintings. This is really cool!"

"What do they look like," called the voices from above.

"I can't really see, I need more light! Plus my head hurts like crazy and I've got blood in my eyes."

"Blood! Holy Crap! I'm going to get Dad," a voice said and then it was quiet.

"SAMSON," another voice called out. It was Thisbe.

"This is Thisbe." She seemed to be crying so the words weren't coming out very clearly.

"Castilia and Wylde went to get Dad. I can see you. Hold on. They'll be right back," Thisbe croaked. She was trying to be strong but he could tell she was scared.

"I'm OK Thiz…don't worry. Do we have the flashlights up there?" Samson said in a stronger voice.

He hated to see his sisters cry, even when he was the cause of it, especially if they were frightened.

Thisbe looked around. "I don't think so... I mean, no. Wylde had them in his backpack and he took off with them. Would you like a sandwich? That's all I have."

"No thanks, but if you have a rag or a bandana, that would be cool." He said.

"I've got the cloth napkins for the picnic," she answered.

"That'll do, throw them down."

Thisbe threw the napkins down and he gathered them and pressed them against his head. Man, did that hurt.

"Thiz, I need some water. I'm really thirsty," he said after the throbbing subsided.

"OK."

Thisbe tied the water bottle to the rope she had brought for the picnic she made and lowered it down. It only made it about half way.

"It's not going to reach." She said.

"Just drop it. I think I'll be able to catch it."

Thisbe dropped the rope and Samson was not even close to catching it. The water bottle landed in the mossy pit with a thud. Samson picked it up and drank the cool water. It was the best water he ever had. It was even better than that fancy french water his grandmother drank out of the blue glass bottle. It made him feel much better.

For an underground cavern, the room was rather warm. Samson was always warm; he really didn't ever get cold. He would typically be barefoot well into fall and winter until his mother made him put on shoes, usually when snow covered the ground.

"Samson!" His Dad called out. "Are you OK?"

"Yeah! I just cut my head. It's not too bad."

"What have you gotten yourself into now? I'm going to throw this rope down. Put the loop around your chest and arms and we'll pull you up."

Samson's Dad threw down the rope and he did as he was instructed. They quickly pulled him up and out of the underground room. The sunlight was blinding and everyone gasped as he was finally pulled out of the hole. Thisbe renewed her crying in full force. Samson's head and blonde hair were covered in blood and it ran down the front of his shirt. He was pale and covered in dirt and mud. He looked like a zombie. Dad had the ATV up on top of the knoll and helped him over to it just about the time Castilia made it back at full sprint with Wylde not far behind.

"I'm going to get him home, you three get back as soon as you can," Dad said as he sped away.

CHAPTER 2

The Presleys

No one would ever doubt that the Presley children where brothers and sisters. Most people assumed they were quadruplets. Except for the slight size difference because of age, they were each a year apart, this was an easy mistake to make. They all had long, very blonde hair, blue eyes, and pale skin. A Presley could be spotted in a crowd fairly easily. Their similar ages made them excellent playmates, well, most of the time. They all had their moments, but generally got along very well for siblings. Samson was the oldest at twelve and liked to wear his hair shoulder length. He had an athletic build and was a solid muscular boy. They all sported the Presley chin dimple of which Samson's was the most prominent. He had many friends and was well liked - this was attributed to the fact that he hated to be alone. He was generally the leader of the pack, which caused some friction with Castilia who was next in line but very much desired to be the oldest. This was probably because Castilia had the most self confidence in the group and could not figure out why or how her parents did not have her first.

She excelled at anything she put her mind to and was therefore a natural at school. Castilia thought herself to be exceptionally pretty, which in fact she was, however, Mom and Dad tried to keep vanity at bay. She was skinny with long arms and legs and broad shoulders: she had a swimmers body.

Castilia and her younger sister Thisbe both had beautiful blonde hair. Thisbe would remind you that her hair has wisps of auburn, which Castilia's did not, making her hair much superior to just plain blonde. Thisbe was a quiet and contemplative child and could spend hours working by herself drawing or painting or reading. She was eager to please and happy to go along on adventures as long as she had a good snack. She was a bit softer than the others, but always had a bright smile. Golden freckles spotted her nose and cheeks when the weather warmed.

The baby, Wylde, hated being called the baby. So he generally tried to disprove this notion by being the bravest of the group. He was always up for a challenge and could be a bit reckless. He could be considered quiet, but that was because he was the youngest and often couldn't get a word in. He was big for his age and solid as the earth. He loved to be outside, digging in the dirt, which seemed to cling to him like paint. One would think he wasn't as fair skinned as his siblings because of the layer of dirt that constantly covered his body.

Castilia, Thisbe and Wylde quickly gathered their things and headed down the path their father had sped down. The dogs were baying at the edge of the yard as they approached and yapped at their heels to the back porch. By the time they made it inside after the accident, Dad had taken Samson to the emergency room. Mom said the cut on his forehead was pretty deep and he was going to need stitches. She did not look pleased. Then the third degree began.

Castilia being the oldest present explained that Samson had gathered everyone up this morning to go on one of his adventures. It being a nice spring day and the weekend, everyone agreed that an adventure was just what was needed. Samson's love of nature and adventures was legend. The long New England winters kept him cooped up inside, most of this time in school, which to Samson's mind was more like prison. He daydreamed his way through boring math and grammar lessons; swashbuckling adventures in warmer climes. History and Science, however, garnered his full attention, as those subjects fueled his adventurous daydreaming. He loved learning of the heroic actions of historic figures and the technology of how things work and how they are made. When the birds began to sing and the winter thaw began to dry out, Samson's shoes were continually lost in some flower bed by the house as he raced from the school bus to the expansive freedom of the backyard. Wylde was typically only a few steps behind. Samson's enthusiasm was so infectious that his sisters, usually against their better judgment, would get caught up in this excitement and join in the fun until such time Castilia would announce there was homework to be done. Much to everyone's chagrin, they would slowly make their way back to the house.

That morning, Thisbe packed a nice picnic and made everyone's favorite sandwiches, including a honey sandwich for Castilia, and collected plenty of snacks for the trip. Wylde gathered all of the tools they might need: flashlight, spade, map, saw, knife, rope, net, insect collector and small animal cage. Castilia made sure she was wearing just the right outfit for an adventure;

a pastel tank top with complementing wide neck t-shirt over it and slightly revealing one shoulder more than the other, completed with daisy shorts and flip flops. The hairstyles varied day to day and mostly depended on whether or not they remembered to brush their hair the night before - if they forgot they found the pain unbearable getting tangles out and a pony tail was all they could manage. Samson made the plan. They were all out of the house before 7 AM as the spring sun was warming the air.

The Presley family lived on a small farm in Connecticut among rolling hills and old stone walls. The farm was 25 acres of bucolic New England landscape nestled next to the western branch of the Saugatuck River. Maple, Ash, Walnut, and Elm trees covered most of the property, with a few large Norway spruces scattered about. It was no longer a real working farm unless you counted the 15 chickens, three dogs, two cats, snake, toad, gerbil, two hamsters and the small garden that Mom and Dad struggled to keep during the summer. The cleared rolling farmland had reverted back to its forested state many years before. The property was littered with farm relics and trash buried in the neglected soil. These relics made for great discoveries and archeological digs. The children loved to explore the property and knew every inch of it by heart.

They were headed toward the orchard at Old Mill Pond to have a picnic. On the way they would stop off at the old knoll where the huge ancient oak tree stood to search for antiquities, tools, scraps of metal, dinosaur bones or old bottles - whatever popped up. They would also spend some time trying to touch the sky in the old oak tree whose expansive limbs made for easy climbing. The knoll was a small smooth rise in a relatively flat area of landscape with dozens of small maple trees on the top, just past the third stone wall on the west side of the property. After they passed under the oak tree and were traversing the top of the knoll, Wylde hit something with the butt of the shovel he was carrying. The ground echoed a huge thump. This was unusual as the earth typically did not make this sound. It made everyone stop in their tracks.

'Thump!" Wylde slammed his shovel down in the spot again.

"There's something under here," Wylde said and excitedly started digging.

"We've finally discovered the treasure of Montezuma!" Samson declared.

Castilia looked at him like he was crazy. "Don't be stupid. Montezuma was the Aztec emperor killed by the Spanish 500 years ago. We're not in Mexico."

"Just think of it," Samson smiled, "riches beyond your wildest dreams!"

Thisbe looked at Samson, then at Castilia. She smiled at Samson and said, "Yay! I want a diamond tiara."

Castilia rolled her eyes, but then added, "If anyone gets a tiara, it will be me."

Wylde, ignoring the conversation between his siblings, continued digging until he uncovered a round wooden plank about the size of a wagon wheel. It looked like a hatch of some sort. He took the shovel and knocked on the top. Thunk, thunk, thunk. Using his hands he began clearing the top, trying to find a way to open the mysterious door. On every side he cleared he found that the wood and the earth meshed into one, becoming a part of each other. After working up a good sweat Wylde screamed in frustration, "There is no way to open this thing!"

"There's nothing under that," Samson said, "be careful."

"Don't be such a worry wart," said Wylde as he began furiously jumping up and down on the top.

"Don't do that!" Samson said and pushed Wylde off the top while moving onto it himself.

The wooden hatch made a very unnatural groan.

"WHAT THA?.." CRASH!!!

CHAPTER 3

Gone

Samson and Dad returned late that afternoon. Samson had gotten 6 stitches for his trouble and a large bandage around his head. The Doctor feared he had a concussion so he was relegated to the bed for the rest of the day and would have to return to the doctor in a week. Until then he was to take it easy. That was like telling a dog not to scratch his fleas.

Dad took Wylde off on the ATV to cover the hole so no one would hurt themselves again, but returned about an hour later astonished that the hole was nowhere to be found. They had combed the whole of the knoll to no avail. It had simply disappeared.

Samson slept the rest of the day and woke the next morning to the smell of Dad's famous blueberry pancakes. He was famished. He suddenly realized he had not eaten anything since yesterday morning. His head was throbbing slightly and his body ached but he pulled himself out of bed, found his robe, and hobbled downstairs, driven by the sweet smell of bacon and pancakes.

When he got to the kitchen everyone was already eating and asked him how he was doing.

"Hungry," he mumbled.

"Well, at least the fall didn't knock out your appetite," said Mom as she fixed him a large stack of pancakes and just the right amount of homemade maple syrup.

After two helpings, he started to slow down. Wylde leaned over and said," You know the hole was gone yesterday when we went back to cover it up."

"What do you mean 'gone'?" Samson asked wiping syrup from his chin.

"I mean 'Gone'. It just disappeared. Dad and I couldn't find it anywhere. I must have dug about a hundred holes looking for it".

"It's true," said Dad. "We must have looked for over an hour. It really wasn't there."

"Ha ha ha, very funny. I guess I just imagined I fell and busted my head." Samson began to get irritated.

"Take it easy. We must have missed it somehow. We'll go back out with Castilia and Thisbe today and check it out," Dad said in a calm, reassuring voice.

It was not uncommon for this sort of tomfoolery to happen in the Presley household. Samson would not put it past his Dad to pull his leg for hours, but when he used his serious Dad voice you knew he wasn't kidding.

Samson was sentenced to a day indoors with his throbbing head. It killed him to see everyone run outside to find the hole without him, but his head was beginning to hurt again so he slowly climbed the stairs to lie down for a while. Almost as soon as he laid down on his bed, he fell into a deep, dream-filled sleep.

He was flying again over the house and the property. The dogs were chasing him from below and barking like mad. The chickens scattered under some brush as if trying to escape a hawk. The cool air washed his face as he sped through the air. His head didn't hurt anymore. He could see the knoll ahead. He circled it a few times looking for the oculus to the dome below. He couldn't find it. He dove to get a better look but suddenly started falling out of the sky. He looked down and saw the gaping hole of the oculus which he fell into heading straight for the bottom of the tomb. He awoke with a start. "Ouch." The sudden jerk hurt his whole body. He had to lie still for a moment to catch his breath. His head was throbbing again. He needed some aspirin. When he got downstairs, Dad had the map on the dining room table and everyone was gathered around. They were pointing and discussing something.

"What's up?" he said quietly.

They all looked up and stared at him for a moment before everyone started talking excitedly at once.

"Too loud…ouch," he said and sat down and cradled his head in his hands.

They all rushed over. After giving Samson some Motrin and water, Thisbe explained that they had been out to the knoll all morning and could not locate the door. It was inexplicable. They had given up. It simply was not there anymore.

Samson rested for the next couple of days and took it slow. School was just as boring as ever and a huge waste of time as it was the last week before summer vacation and nothing of any importance was being done. It was a fine time to sit back and let things heal. Samson could not wait for the weekend so he could head back up to the knoll and find that blasted door. In the meantime, he tried to draw out some of the pictures he had seen in the tomb. He wasn't a bad artist but nothing he drew looked too familiar. It had been too dark and he had been too hurt.

"Fire," Thisbe said looking over his shoulder.

"What?" Samson looked at her.

"You keep on drawing fire," she said with a smile and floated off.

*   *   *

School got out for the summer that week and as a result things were quite hectic around the Presley house as they are when freedom reigns supreme. Everyone was preoccupied with saying good bye to close friends and readying themselves for two months of unorganized anarchistic unfettered ignorance; or at least that was the plan. Samson even forgot that he had to go to the doctor to have his stitches removed and to check his concussion. More importantly he had even forgotten about the mysterious disappearance of the entry to the tomb. The last days of school were always filled with a mad frenzy to sign and come up with witty "see you next year" aphorisms to tattoo year books. Most of the local kids would pack up their worldly belonging and head off to summer camp in Maine or upstate New York. The Presley kids, however, were destined to an average summer devout of archery lessons, sailing adventures, and constant sleepovers. They would be bored to tears wasting the precious summer hours at home. It was a cruel fate but one that Mom strongly believed in. It seemed the harder they pleaded or begged to be sent away to camp the more resolved she was to keep everyone under the same roof. Sending kids off to camp during the only time of the year that the family could actually be together without the constant burden of running one kid or the other off to a sport or music lesson was sacrosanct.

At this point in time, everyone knew not to ask about summer sleep away camps in fear of severe retribution, however, everyone was allowed a week of an organized summer camp that involved some specific interest. Samson, who since the age of one could rarely be found without a toy airplane in hand simulating a flight around the yard, was enrolled in an airplane camp at a local airstrip. Castilia was joining the junior achievement academy and would spend a week visiting local museums. Thisbe chose to work on her grace and flexibility at a week-long gymnastics camp. Wylde was doing an adventure camp that included cave exploration and rock climbing. The rest of the summer was to be spent visiting the beach and working out in the yard and completing a laundry list of chores that accumulated throughout the school year around the property. The Presley kids were virtual slaves on Fox Hollow Farm. Their main summer objective was to avoid as much work as possible while maintaining the appearance of being responsible and productive young people. It was a delicate balance, but after a few years of the same routine they were masterful participants.

One lazy summer morning when Mom had taken Wylde to get some new climbing shoes and Castilia had managed to score a sleepover, Samson and Thisbe decided it was time to revisit the site of the accident and see for themselves if the opening did indeed vanish. The morning was cool and the sky was blue. It was a perfect day to avoid cleaning the chicken coop. Thisbe packed some snacks and peanut butter and honey sandwiches even though they didn't expect to be out long. Mom would be home soon and they would be forced into some chore at some point way before lunch. However, the longer they could stay away from the house, the longer their reprieve would last. They reached the knoll in no time and began an exhaustive search for the tomb entry.

"It's got to be along this path," Samson began, "we were hiking to the pond when Wylde hit the door with the shovel. Did you bring that by the way?"

"What? I brought sandwiches." Thisbe replied in disbelief. She had fulfilled her duties perfectly. "Anyway, I didn't walk up here to dig a bunch of holes and get all dirty and sweaty."

"Ok, ok… well, you look on the right side of the path and I'll look on the left."

After about 15 minutes of searching, Samson found a spot that looked fairly disturbed but there was no door or hole. "I think that's my blood right there." He said to Thisbe.

"Ooowa. Gross." Thisbe scrunched up her nose but then said, " oh, I think you are right…it trails over to here where the ATV tracks are, but that doesn't make any sense. We pulled you out of the hole then got you immediately on the ATV. The hole should be right beside that bush."

"Clearly, it's not. So what happened to it?" Samson pondered. He didn't have long to think about it as the bell his mother used to call the children home was ringing incessantly in the air. "Crap, I guess it's time to shovel some chicken poo. Let's go."

"But, what about the sandwiches?" Thisbe said with a frown.

"Later," Samson said. "Race you back." He took off down the dusty path.

"Hey, wait for me!!" Thisbe shoved the sandwiches back in her pack and trotted after Samson. He was nowhere to be seen. The boy was fast. Sometimes it looked as if he was actually flying and his feet were not touching the ground. She was no slouch when it came to running but her style was more laid back. Like most things, she liked to glide along flowing like the wind, which is exactly what she did.

The rest of the day was spent cleaning this and that, much to the dismay of the four participants, and they ended their day with an afternoon trip to the beach for a summer picnic with Dad meeting them there after work. The next few days were spent in much the same fashion, summer cleaning and getting ready for camps the following week.

CHAPTER 4

The Chamber

They didn't have any time to explore again until a couple of days later when they found themselves with no chores left to do and Mom had to go out to the local farmer's market for groceries. They all decided to go down to the pond and see how the fishing was.

They worked as a team to get the things they needed for a morning outing. Samson got the rods and the tackle, Wylde dug up some worms, the dogs loved to help him do this and swarmed around him sticking their nose into each hole he dug. Thisbe took care of the food and Castilia made sure everyone had their rubber boots except for her- she had just gotten these cute new white sneakers she was just dying to wear so she opted for these instead. She was just going to watch anyway. Mom said she wouldn't be long and to come home for lunch and they would decide what to do for the afternoon. They dutifully agreed to be back then and took off toward the pond, once again traversing the knoll. Wylde had brought the shovel and bucket as he didn't find enough worms around the house and would look for more by the pond. Approaching the knoll they had all but forgotten about the tomb and hole as they started past the old oak tree and hiked up to the apex.

"Thunk!"

Everyone froze.

"Oh my Gosh." Castilia said in a whisper.

"Thunk, thunk." Wylde hit the ground again with the shovel. He looked at Samson who nodded to him. Wylde placed his backpack and bucket on the ground and started digging. The other three ran over and began pushing dirt away from the area with their hands. It took just a few seconds to uncover the wooded door a second time.

"Now what do we do?" Wylde said, staring down at the door. His eyes wide with wonder.

"We're going to need some rope," Samson started.

"And some flashlights," Castilia said.

"And a camera," Wylde continued.

"We're definitely going to need some more sandwiches," Thisbe said with a smile and they all burst out laughing as they ran back to the house as fast as their legs could carry them.

They had gotten a hammer and a crowbar from their Dad's shop and managed to pry open the door. It did, in fact, open rather easily.

"I wish we would have done that last time," Samson said rubbing his forehead. They looked down into the dark hole.

"Who's going in first?" Samson asked warily looking at Castilia.

"I'll go," Castilia said. She was always the first to volunteer for any unknown task. She had no fear when it came to things like this, much to the relief of everyone else, except Wylde, who also liked to dive in head first but being the youngest, he vary rarely had the first opportunity. Samson usually regained his courage after Castilia initially checked things out and therefore was the second. Thisbe was perfectly happy going last.

"It would be really helpful to have a tree nearby to tie the rope onto," said Wylde and looked around.

"Too bad there doesn't…." He began, "Oh… here's a nice big maple right behind me. Hum…I can't believe I didn't notice that before."

They all looked a little startled. In fact, none of them had noticed that tree before. It was almost if the tree snuck up behind them as if called to action. Wylde secured the climbing rope to the tree using a figure eight knot he had learned at the indoor rock climbing gym they often visited in the winter. Samson tested it to everyone's approval and then threw the rope down into the hole. They gave Castilia a LED headlamp and she started toward the hole.

"Wait a minute… How am I going to get out of there? If that hole is as deep as it was before, I won't be able to climb all the way out of the hole."

"We'll all stay up here and pull you up when you are ready," Samson said. "Here, take your itouch and take a bunch of pictures."

"If you're going to be up here then why don't you lower me down too? I might fall if I have to take too much stuff."

"OK, that's a better idea. Are you sure you want to do this?" Samson looked doubtful.

"If all three of you are on the rope, I should be ok. Both you and Thisbe can pick me up on your own and Wylde is not too far behind. Plus I'm the lightest one out of all of us, even

Wylde has gotten heavier than me." Castilia said looking over to Wylde.

"It's all muscle, baby. You all know Boom and Bang," he said flexing then kissing his two semi-muscular biceps that he had so affectionately named.

"OK then let's pull up the rope and I can make a harness for you. We'll wrap the rope around the tree to create a break so it will be easy to lower you down slowly and make sure we can stop you if needed." Samson explained.

They pulled up the rope and made a harness around Castilia's waist and legs and then wrapped the rope around the tree. They took a length of rope and tied it off higher on the tree that they guessed was the total depth of the hole as a stop gap against any loose hands. Castilia sat on the edge of the opening and looked down into the darkness. Samson, Wylde and Thisbe all grabbed the rope and looked anxiously at her.

Castilia smiled a sly smile and slid her butt off the edge and she gave a yelp when she fell a couple of feet into the hole. The rope held and the others did not yet really feel the pull of her weight.

"OK, lower me down." Castilia said confidently.

They all loosened their grip and the rope slid slowly around the tree and down into the hole. The set up seemed to be working and they all relaxed a bit. They managed to get her down to the bottom of the tomb without any trouble.

"Almost there, Slow down!" Castilia said at last. Then they heard her scream.

It wasn't a blood curdling scream, more of a startled scream, but a scream nonetheless. They all tensed and pulled tight on the rope and held their breath.

"WHAT'S WRONG! ARE YOU OK?" Samson yelled at the hole, sweating profusely now and extremely worried.

"I'm ok", Castilia yelled back up. "I landed in a pool of water down here and its freezing. I think I've ruined these pants. Anyway, it's not deep, just a few inches. Give me some slack and I can walk around."

Castilia got up and surveyed the room. It was as Samson described, a huge domed room with the circular opening at the center of the ceiling. She looked down and was standing in a pool of water in the center circle that Samson said was dry. Oh this was just great, now her nice new summer shoes were wet and dirty. She hoped her Mom wouldn't get too mad, but she knew it would be a while before she would be able to get white tennis shoes again. This was a disaster, now her white shoes would be permanently stained and wouldn't match any of her outfits. It's a good thing most of her friends were away at summer camp, but she was supposed to go to the movies on Friday with some girls that were still in town. Maybe Mom knew how to wash them.

"What do you see down there?" Samson called down jolting Castilia out of her thoughts and back to the matter at hand.

"Oh, hold on." She said as she turned the flashlight on and started to look around. "Wow."

"What?"

It took Castilia a few moments to look around and take it all in. She slowly stepped out of the pool and gazed around at the walls.

"What do you see?"

"It's really pretty. There are all these paintings on the walls. They look really familiar but I can't think of where I've seen them before. There are four murals that encircle the room. This first one looks like a huge fire and is surrounded by smoke and what looks like volcanoes. The next looks like the sea as it is surrounded by all sorts of fish, whales, squid, seals – you name it. I guess the next one is storms or something as it has a picture of a tornado and clouds but surrounded by birds. The last one must be land. It shows mountains and trees and all kinds of animals. It's very well done. It doesn't look like typical cave paintings at all, more like Michelanglo."

"Who? What did she say?" said Wylde

"She just said her brain is real big," Thisbe said rolling her eyes.

"Take some pictures," they yelled down.

"Oh right." She said as she pulled her itouch out of her back pocket to discover that it was a bit waterlogged from her dip in the pool. "OH POO! It's not working. It got wet!"

Castilia could hear the bell ringing from inside the tomb.

"We've got to get back home. We'll pull you up. Walk back to the center." Samson called down.

Castilia splashed back into the pool and looked up at her brother's and sister's faces peering down at her. They disappeared and the rope became taut. Her feet left the water and she looked around as she made her ascent and tried to remember everything she could see.

CHAPTER 5

The Elements

One look at Castilia and Mom blew her top. Castilia spent the rest of the day cleaning her new shoes and the rest of the laundry in the house. The others were distracted with other things until about bedtime when Wylde came to Samson with a print of a rope ladder he downloaded off of the internet.

"If we had one of these, we could all get down there. Do you think you can help me make it?" he said.

"We'll need a lot of rope, but I think Dad has plenty in the barn. We'll go check it out in the morning and see what we can do. Great idea, little bro!" Samson said with a smile.

Early the next morning, as promised, the brothers raided the barn and found a few good lengths of rope. They knew Dad wouldn't like his rope being pilfered, but this clearly was worth the risk. They took the rope, hid it in the tree house, and then spent the next few days making the ladder. They tested sections of it by tying it outside the tree house and climbing down. It only failed once, but luckily Wylde was only about two rungs from the ground when the knot gave way.

"Epic Fail!" Samson yelled from above, laughing.

Even though Wylde did hurt himself from the fall and was pushing back the tears as he dusted himself off, Samson's obnoxious comment made him laugh. He scrapped his knee a bit but it wasn't bleeding much and plus the dirt was keeping most of the blood from running down his leg. He scrambled back up the tree and they continued working.

In the meantime, Castilia was busy doing a little research on the internet and made a fantastic discovery. She called to Thisbe in the next room who was busy choreographing some dance moves to a song she heard on the radio and couldn't get out of her head. Thisbe floated over and cartwheeled beside Castilia.

"This has got to be it," Castilia said excitedly, "it's exactly like what I saw. What do you think?"

"What does this mean?" Thisbe said as she read.

"I don't know, but it can't be a coincidence." Castilia printed out the page and they hurried to the treehouse which had become the operational headquarters.

"I found it, I found it," she said breathlessly as her head popped into the treehouse.

"Found what? Some sense? It's about time." Wylde said laughing.

"No silly, I think I found what the pictures mean in the tomb." Castilia said with a stern look. Boys could be so immature. "I can't believe how easy it was in the end. I started by going to the library and looking at history books of cave paintings which led to absolutely nothing, and then I flipped through some art books which proved to be equally useless. So I came home and just googled 'fire, sea, storm and land.' And up pops this Wikipedia listing for the 'four elements.'" She continued holding up the paper. " The four elements have roots in just about every civilization, past and present. Instead of fire, sea, storm and land, the four elements are fire, water, air and earth; exactly what I saw depicted in the murals. These four elements are thought to be the simplest essential parts of basically everything. Combined with the fifth element, they have the power of creation."

"What is the fifth element?" Samson asked

"That's the really interesting part. No one really knows. The Greeks called it 'Aether.' The Hindus called it 'Akash.' The Japanese called it the 'Void.' Native Americans called it 'Wanagi.' Every culture has some version of the five elements, but they are all fundamentally the same," she said.

"So you think this tomb is actually some sort of temple?" Samson said.

"I have no idea, but I think we may have stumbled onto something really big. Bigger than the treasure of Montezuma." Castilia said with a huge smile.

*   *   *

The next day they were all quite excited to visit the knoll once again. Unfortunately, Castilia had a dentist appointment that morning but urged the other three to go on without her to find the temple. She would catch up with them as soon as she got back.

Samson, Wylde and Thisbe packed up the rope ladder and all of their gear and headed up to the knoll as soon as Mom left with Castilia. They followed the path just as they had done on their previous outings. When they passed the big oak tree they all began poking at the ground with walking sticks.

They proceeded like this all the way around the knoll without any luck.

"Wait a minute!" Wylde yelled. "I don't have the shovel. Maybe the shovel is what finds the door." He promptly dropped his gear and ran down the path toward the house. When he returned a few minutes later with the shovel he was out of breath and handed the shovel to Thisbe to begin looking for the door. She vigorously combed the hill banging the butt of the shovel on the ground in increasing frustration. "Where the HECK is it?" she finally yelled throwing the shovel to the ground.

"You know, Wylde found the door both times before. Maybe he has to do it? Here, give it a shot." Samson said picking up the shovel and handing it to Wylde.

Wylde spent the next fifteen minutes pounding the ground with the shovel just as his sister had done to no avail and he too threw the shovel down in disgust.

"I don't get it," Thisbe said, "Why can't we find the stupid door? Is it gone for good now?"

After taking a break and scratching their heads, Samson gave it a half-hearted go but was thwarted as well. They had begun to pack it up when Castilia made it to the knoll and asked what they were doing.

"We can't find the stupid door." Wylde said with a red face. "We've looked all over this stupid hill, poked and prodded every inch of it and still can't find it. We don't understand it." He stood up and jerked up the shovel.

"Really, if I remember right, it should be where we dug that hole by the maple tree." He pointed over to the hole by a nearby maple tree. "I just don't understand it," he started getting more agitated and raising his voice as he continued to rant. "We've looked all over this knoll and it's nowhere to be found! This is crazy! I'm tired and I'm going home!" he yelled slamming the butt of the shovel into the dirt.

"THUNK!"

They all jumped.

"WHAT THE HECK!!!" Wylde screamed in frustration as he started digging ferociously. The others ran over to the spot and helped clear the dirt off of the door.

"I don't understand it. How come we couldn't find it all morning?" Thisbe said with a frown.

"Listen. The only times we've found this door is when we are all together," Samson said thoughtfully. "Castilia just walked up so we were able to find it. When she was gone this morning we couldn't."

"Makes a whole lotta sense big brother," Castilia replied. "We'll have to test that theory in the future but now I think it's time to check out this temple."

They fastened the rope ladder on a tree outside of the hole. Wylde noticed that the tree was not the same one they had used to lower Castilia down the last time. It was an ash tree, not a maple. In fact the hole seemed to be in a totally different location. The others were skeptical, but Wylde knew his trees and it definitely was a sugar maple before, and this was an ash. Either the hole was moving, or the trees were, or both.

Castilia took the lead and made it down to the bottom of the temple and once again stepped into the shallow pool. "Ugh," she moaned as her white shoes soaked up the moisture. It took her a whole day to clean these shoes the last time. Why couldn't she remember to wear her Bogs when they did things like this? Mom was going to kill her...again. Samson was the next to descend. He jumped off the ladder and landed in the pool, splashing muddy water all over Castilia, who was gazing up at the paintings.

"What the HECK, Samson!" she screamed. "Great, just great. Now Mom is REALLY going to kill me."

"Sorry," Samson said with a mischievous grin.

Wylde and Thisbe followed and gasped as they got their footing and were able to look around.

"It's beautiful." Thisbe said, awestruck.

"I told you." Castilia said. "So that must be Fire," she said pointing at the elaborately decorative composition directly in front of them, "and Water and Wind and Earth." She continued rotating and pointing as she spoke. They all wandered around the temple gazing up at the elaborate composition and didn't speak for many minutes.

"I like this one," Thisbe said pointing up to the Wind collage. "It is calm and peaceful but strong and powerful at the same time."

"No, this one is the best," Castilia said pointing at the picture of the sea. "It is the majestic ocean that covers the majority of the earth. It reminds me of our trips to the beach and how much fun we had."

"Did you see these volcanoes!" Samson roared. "Kaplush!" he made an explosion sound with his mouth.

"You need to come see this!" Wylde said over the explosion. "It is the coolest one ever! It's got mountains and trees and all sorts of animals."

They all began talking and shouting at once, extolling the virtues of their chosen composition. The gracious admiration quickly devolved into a torrent of insults about how stupid all of the other paintings were. It was a cacophony of inventive slanders bouncing off the domed walls that could have awakened the dead.

"Fire is stupid. All you have to do is pour water on it and it goes out!" Castilia yelled.

"Are you crazy! Fire will turn water to steam and burn up all of the stupid fish and it totally burns all of the trees."

"Earth does not burn and will smother fire. It can also cover water."

"What? Don't be stupid. Water turns earth to mud."

"Then dries up and earth is still there."

Only Thisbe stayed out of the fray as she was wont to do. She calmly looked up at the painting and let the noise float past her.

"Earth and Fire are both stupid and you are too…," Castilia said, well into the heat of the argument, when something caught her eye. "What's that?" she said pointing at Samson.

"Oh no, don't try to distract me now, I've got you right where I want you. Fire is so much more powerful…" Samson retorted.

"No really, what is that glowing under your shirt?" she said still pointing at his chest.

Samson looked down and saw that something was indeed glowing under his shirt. He pulled out the necklace he was wearing around his neck.

"It's the amulet Granddad gave me for my birthday last year-it's glowing," he said pulling it over his head. He placed it in his hand and stared at it. The others approached to get a better look.

Samson's Granddad had given him this necklace on his twelfth birthday, saying that it was a special medallion that he got in Vietnam when he was over there during the War. He claimed the medallion actually found him when he was in Vietnam before he was sent out in the field of duty. He never usually talked about the War or what he did there, but he explained that the day he arrived an elderly Vietnamese woman excitedly came up to him and spoke quickly in a language he did not understand. She repeated "Toi de tim thay ban," over and over again, and pressed the medallion in his hand. She was crying as he left and held her hand to her heart and smiled a toothless smile as he waved to her and hung the medallion around his neck. He figured it was just some welcoming ritual by the natives. Once he had gotten to the base, he asked a translator there what "Toi de tim thay ban" meant. The translator shrugged and said, "It means 'I've found you.'" He then asked a few other soldiers if they had gotten a necklace as well but no one knew what he was talking about. Granddad said he didn't really think much of it but liked the look of the medallion and it felt nice around his neck so he kept it. He had four tours of duty and was in many fire fights. He saw countless men die beside him, but he always came back alive and unscathed. He thought the woman was an angel and the medallion was his lucky talisman.

After the war, it was years before he felt comfortable taking it off for any period of time. He often thought about passing it on to one of his daughters but it didn't feel right. Then he met his first grandchild. The day he visited the hospital, Samson was apparently not very comfortable and had been crying for most of the night. He walked into the maternity ward and heard Samson's healthy lungs filling the air with cries. His daughter and son-in-law were very exhausted, upset and exasperated and had put the baby in the bassinet to give themselves a break.

Grandad bent down over the bassinet and saw a beet red little scream machine wailing to no one in particular. He picked him up to try and sooth him and held him tight against his chest. He could feel the baby's tense body relax almost immediately and the crying stopped. Samson's parents were, of course, flabbergasted and looked at him dumbstruck. Being as exhausted as they were, they did not comment or protest. They almost immediately fell asleep in the silence.

It was then that Grandad noticed a red glow in his shirt. His talisman was glowing and warm against his skin. Samson opened his eyes wide, looked at his grandfather, smiled, then went calmly to sleep. The talisman chose its successor that day. He hoped his angel would now look over his grandson.

The talisman in Samson's hand was round, about the size of a quarter. It was a grey metal and had elaborate carving on it that weaved around and resembled a flame in the center. It looked very Celtic. It was currently glowing an iridescent red. This was all very strange and a little creepy, however, Samson felt a great calm come over his body. He felt stronger and older and looked at his brother and sisters there in the dark tomb. He did love them more than he could say. Thisbe was clearly getting nervous. It was obvious that she was frightened and was on the verge of crying. Samson decided it was time to go.

"Let's get out of here," Samson said breaking the silence. "This is too creepy."

"Oh my Gosh, you are reading my mind," Thisbe said as she hurried to the ladder. She was up and gone before the others had even moved.

"She can really move fast when she wants to," Wylde observed with a snicker as they watched Thisbe disappear through the oculus. Wylde and Samson laughed until the sight of the consternation on Castilia's face reminded them of their current predicament.

"OK," Samson said as he and Wylde sobered. "What's up with you?"

"This is really weird. We need to tell Mom and Dad." Castilia said.

"Are you crazy?" Samson replied. "They'll never believe any of this."

"Well, your necklace is glowing and we're standing in a magic underground stone dome that we can only find when we are together. This seems like it's way out of our league, don't ya think?"

After Samson and Wylde begrudgingly acknowledged that their sister had a point, the three resolved to show their parents the pictures and tell them about this place as soon as they could. Wylde took out the camera and took several more pictures around the temple as they gathered their stuff to leave. They each climbed the rope ladder up and out of the oculus and headed home a little stunned by what they had discovered.

CHAPTER 6

Fox Hollow

Mom had cooked a great meal as usual for dinner. She had worked up her famous shrimp and grits. It was a Presley family favorite. The family always tried to have dinner together as much as possible to review the day and let Dad know what was going on. They were all very hungry after the day's adventure and enjoyed the meal in virtual silence.

"Mom, Dad, we have something to talk to you about," Samson began.

"OK. What cha got?" Dad answered curiously.

"You know the hole I fell in at the top of the knoll…" Samson started.

"Samson. I thought I told you not to go up there again. That place is dangerous. You could get seriously hurt if you fell in there again." Dad scolded.

"But we couldn't find it. You couldn't find it. We thought it was gone. You have to admit it is a huge mystery. How could we let that go?"

"I'll give you that. So did you find it again?" Dad said with a slight grin.

"Sam please. You're only encouraging them and they certainly don't need any encouragement." Mom urged.

"We did find it!" Wylde said. He could hardly contain himself. "We made a rope ladder this time and got down there without a problem, even though the hole was in a different place and we had to tie the ladder to a different tree which is really weird and the walls were covered with cool paintings and Samson's necklace started to glow so we got freaked out and..."

"Hold on, Hold on. Better start at the beginning." Dad said confused.

Castilia then took up the story of how they found the hole the second time and that she really ruined her shoes down there and not in the river like she told Mom, "sorry Mom". Her mother scowled at her but let her continue the story, including her research and their ideas of the four elements. At last she finished her story with the glowing necklace. Mom and Dad sat there for a minute, wide-eyed and took it all in.

"Wow, that's some story. You said you have pictures," Dad said.

"Yes sir," Wylde said as he got up to get the camera.

Dad turned on the camera and started flipping though the images.

"All these pictures are dark, I can't see anything except for one or two of you standing in a dark cave." Dad said.

"What? Let me see that." Samson said. He flipped through the digital images and discovered that it was true. The flash on the camera lit up the person in front of the walls. The background was completely dark. They couldn't seem to get a picture of the place. This too was curious.

"I wonder if that is the old Indian burial ground Susie Jenkins was telling me about?" Mom said thoughtfully.

Everyone looked at her curiously

"Well, you all know the story of how we came to own this house." Mom began.

"Oh I love that story, please tell it again," Thisbe said with great anticipation, clapping her hands.

"OK, it is relevant I guess. You all know that we lived in Norwalk when Samson was born and our house there was very small. It had two bedrooms and one bath, which was fine for 2 people and a baby, but we knew we needed more space. Your father and I looked around the area for a year and found nothing we could afford that was bigger than we had. We had to keep looking further and further from the train line to the city to find something affordable. I used to take Samson in the car and we would just wander around back streets and country roads looking for "For Sale" signs. One day we were actually on our way to see another house in Westville and the Subaru got a flat tire right in front of this house. At this time, believe it or not, not everyone had a cell phone, and I was one of those people. So I got Samson out of the car and we walked up to the nearest house to ask to use the phone to call your Dad.

The house was this lovely Victorian farmhouse with its beautiful porches and tall ceilings. We rang the bell and a spry old woman answered the door. She looked at me for a long time with a quizzical expression on her face. I started to explain that our car had a flat tire right out front of her house and I was wondering if we could use her phone when a huge smile grew on her face and she simply said "Well, it's about time, I've been waiting for you. Come in, come in." I was really worried that she was a senile old lady who thought I was someone else, so I tried to explain again about the flat tire and she said "Of course, of course. Come on in and I'll show you the house." Now I was positive that she was senile and said that we just wanted to use the phone. She smiled again and said, "Aren't you looking to buy a house?" I was taken back a bit but said "yes" meekly and she said "that's what I thought; this is the house for you. Come on in." At that point I was thoroughly discombobulated and followed her into the house. I continued my request to use the phone for a few minutes until I really began to look around. The house was, of course, everything we were looking for. We took the whole tour of the house and it was perfect, but it was also obvious that we would never be able to afford it. The old lady said "Nonsense, I've owned this house for over 60 years and paid it off long ago. I've been waiting for you to come and buy it for years." I asked her what she meant by that and she said, "My husband and I bought this house long ago when the previous owner suddenly disappeared. It was fate that brought us to this house and made it available to us. We have loved this house just as much as it has loved us. However, over the years we came to the knowledge that we were simply the stewards of this property. The house and property spoke to us but we knew that it was waiting for someone else. My husband died six years ago and since then I've been waiting on you to come here to buy the house. I actually didn't think it would take this long but it's definitely you."

"I almost took Samson and ran from the house, because this lady was clearly crazy. After more conversation about how she loved the house and raised six children here, it began to dawn on me that the lady, who finally introduced herself as Ms.

Goodwyn, was very lucid. I was finally allowed to call Dad to come and change the tire and see the house. He, as you know, immediately fell in love with the house. We made her an offer on the spot. It was all the money we had to spend and she accepted. Little did we know at the time the property had so much acreage. We didn't have much faith that the deal would go through."

"We waited with bated breath for about a month as the lawyers took over and finalized the contract. We were convinced some relative would show up to protest the sale of the house by saying that Ms. Goodwyn was incompetent. To the contrary, we did meet one of her daughters at the house inspection, who had grandchildren herself and lived just down the road a bit. She said that we had made her mother very happy. She was glad that her mother would finally move out of the old house." Mom continued. "After we moved in, we were very surprised to discover the old mill stone placed by the back door in which was carved the word "Seward," which is my maiden name. It was eerily perfect. We were destined to live in this house. It was serendipity at its finest." Mom smiled and everyone nodded.

"But back to what I was saying about Susie Jenkins. You know she works at the Historical Society. She said that the archives had a map that showed an Indian burial ground on what may be our property. We should go down there and check it out. Perhaps that burial ground is somehow connected to the dome you four are talking about."

After a little more discussion, they all agreed to stay away from the knoll for now until they could get a little more information. They would visit the Historical Society and get a copy of the map and see if they could dig up any more information about the area. It was getting late by the time they finished

talking and everyone helped clean the kitchen then headed up
to bed.

CHAPTER 7

Dr. Lovejoy

The next day was Sunday and Mom was off to church. She convinced Castilia and Thisbe to tag along. The family didn't belong to a church as Mom and Dad were not very religious, however, Mom liked to attend different churches in the area to get different points of view. She didn't discriminate. She tried them all at least once and if it felt right she would return. She figured it was a good idea to cover all of your bases just in case. She also enjoyed the singing and the pomp and circumstance of the ceremony. Today they were to visit the local Second True Congregation of Christ Church, as they had a new preacher who was garnering more than the usual buzz in the social circles, and he apparently gave quite the sermon. The fact that he was not hard on the eyes was an added bonus.

Dr. Leroy Lovejoy had a permanent smile on his face and was always cheerful. He had perfect teeth and he was very proud of them. Perhaps this is why he smiled so much. His kind face radiated confidence and compassion and he always had perfectly quaffed hair with nary a hair out of place. He had a melodic voice that would carry for miles, but was not grating. He always wore a white suit, shirt, tie and shoes to complete the picture. It was a wonder the man was not on television asking viewers to reach deep inside their hearts and pocketbooks to give the church a hand. Even though Dr. Lovejoy was this perfect caricature, his demeanor was very sincere and his sermons very serious.

Today's sermon was "How do you earn God's Love." He preached that one should devote his/her lives to earning God's love as it was the only truly worthy earthy purpose. He explained that earning God's love was easy. Everyone knew how to do it and what to do. Be nice to one another, help one another, strive to be a good person, don't beg, steal or cheat your neighbor. And besides, even if you weren't concerned with reciprocation, wouldn't the world be a better place with more niceness? If everyone in the congregation did one unsolicited nice thing today, the world would be a better place if just for one day, one moment, and isn't that worth doing? He asked at the closing of the sermon. It was a simple sermon but delivered with such precision and depth of feeling that everyone in the congregation was enthralled. After his sermon, the singing was a little louder and the rejoicing a little more positive.

At the end of the service, the blue-haired old ladies, who seemed to dress up a little nicer for church these days, practically climbed over each other to get to Dr. Lovejoy and be the first to shake his hand and speak with him for just a moment. The crowd of ladies was so thick that one could hardly get out of the chapel. Mom often liked to meet the preacher to get a sense of them and to see if she would want to return, but the chances of her fighting off the horde of swooning women was slim to none. Mom and the girls made their way through the crowd and were heading down the steps when a hand softly touched her shoulder. She turned as was startled to see Dr. Lovejoy's smiling face.

"Oh, excuse me but I do like to meet all newcomers to the Church," he said brightly, "I don't believe I've yet had the honor. I'm Dr. Leroy Lovejoy."

Mom was speechless for a moment and just looked at his outstretched hand. He was quite charming and he smelled of lilacs. "Oh, yes," she stuttered, blushing slightly. "I apologize. We were going to come say hello but there was such a crowd around you we thought you would be occupied for some time. I'm Daisy Presley and these are my daughters Castilia and Thisbe."

"Thank you all for coming to the service. I do hope you enjoyed it," He said with another toothy smile.

Before Mom could say anything Castilia said, "It all seemed pretty obvious to me."

Dr. Lovejoy raised his eyebrows in surprise and focused his attention on Castilia, his smile slightly diminished. "Well now, little lady, how do you mean?"

"Of course the world would be a better place if people were nicer. It seems obvious." She said.

"That is very insightful," he retorted, "but if that were the case then why aren't people nicer? That is really the question, isn't it? I bet you think your room looks better when it is clean and there are no clothes on the floor."

"Yes I do," Castilia replied politely.

"Yet I would think if I ask your Mother if you always pick your clothes off the floor she would tell me that you do not and she has to remind you to do it often," he said.

"Very often," Mom grinned.

"It's true, it's true!" Thisbe laughed.

"OK, I'll admit I sometimes don't pick up my clothes, so what?" Castilia consented.

"We all need reminders of the obvious," he said with a wink and his smile grew to an impossible size. "It's wonderful that you came. And it seems you also listened which I greatly appreciate. I hope we'll see you again."

"That is a strong possibility. It was nice meeting you too Dr. Lovejoy, have a nice day," Mom said and began descending the steps as the girls waved goodbye.

Dr. Lovejoy stood on the stairs watching them depart a little longer than usual as he was enveloped by his flock once again.

CHAPTER 8

The Peabody

Camp week started on Monday so no one had time to go by the Historical Society. Mom spent her day shuttling kids to and fro and organizing things for the next day. Samson was off to a Pilot camp at Danbury Airport where they would learn about small four seat planes and fly an actual flight simulator. The camp was set up as a beginner course for young people who might be interested in eventually getting a pilot's license. The week would end with a one-on-one flight with an instructor. The students who were ready would be allowed to fly the plane as the first mate. Samson, of course, was fully expecting to be allowed to take off, do barrel rolls and land the plane on his own by the end of the week, even after the repeated warning from Mom that he would be lucky if he got to steer the plane for a few minutes on the last day.

Castilia was very excited about her museum camp which would visit a new museum every day of the week including The Maritime Aquarium in Norwalk, Yale Art Museum, the Peabody Museum in New Haven, The Bruce Museum in Greenwich, culminating in a trip to the Metropolitan Museum in New York City on Friday. They would be getting VIP treatment complete with special tour name badges, full access to closed exhibits and plenty of behind the scenes presentations on the inner workings of each museum, and hearing lectures, and seeing how the museums worked.

Thisbe had an intensive Gymnastics camp for the week, where they would meet and work with Gabby Douglas, the 2012 Olympic Gold Medalist. Wylde was headed to a weeklong Adventure camp where he would be exploring many different Connecticut ecologies and activities; kayaking in the Long Island Sound, rock climbing near Kent, and hiking at Bear Mountain to name a few.

Everyone enjoyed the first day of camp. Samson, however, was a bit disappointed. "I had no idea learning to fly was so hard. It's like you have to go to another whole school to learn all this stuff.

They didn't even let us sit in a plane today. It was all 'safety this and safety that.' I'm never going to get to fly."

His mother explained, "you know if something goes wrong with a plane you fall out of the sky. That's kind of a big deal. You have a lot to learn." Patience was never Samson's strong point, and neither was school. The two together were painful.

Castilia's camp went to the Peabody Museum of Natural History in New Haven on the third day. The Peabody is housed on the campus of Yale University in what looks to be a stone gothic chapel. It is a nice old museum that has incredible exhibits for its size. It also has the support of Yale University and its staff. Today they would get an added bonus of a lecture by one of Yale's noted archeologists.

The main entry was through a heavy wooden door with a gothic arch. The entry hall and stair was formed with the same brown sandstone that covered the exterior of the building. Hanging above your head as you entered was a life-size replica of a giant squid, it's solitary eye staring down at each an every visitor as they entered the museum. The camp group gathered under its watchful gaze as the museum curator greeted them and began their tour.

The main hall had a wonderfully diverse exhibit of dinosaur bones and other exotic animals. They walked through the single-story exhibit space led by the curator of the museum, who explained the rich history of the Peabody and Yale's involvement in early archeology. They were then brought to the lecture hall to find a rather small thin man standing at the lectern watching them file in with curious eyes. He had a small round nose that was accentuated by his bulbous face and full cheeks that looked like fleshy jowls. His round face was made even more round by his receding hairline and oily dark hair that seemed to be painted on his skull. He had large bulging eyes and wore a pair of bifocal glasses that perched percariously upon his button nose like they were constantly in jeopardy of slipping off . He looked exactly like a scholarly professor, complete with tweed jacket with elbow pads, vest, and a nice red bow tie. Castilia thought he looked a little like a Pug, a very smart Pug. They all marched into the lecture hall and had a seat. He spoke as soon as everyone was seated. Castilia expected his voice to be very biting and nasally like that of a small barking dog, but it was the practiced, clear voice of a grand orator and lecturer. The mere sound of it was erudite.

"Good morning. I am Professor Bartamus Finch, and I am an archeologists. I understand that this group is from Westville and you are visiting several museums this week. I too live in Westville and I welcome you to the Peabody. Secondly, I applaud your intellectual curiosity. When most kids are running around in circles exercising their bodies, you have decided to exercise your minds. I believe that is a bold choice for you to make. I certainly would have made the same choice myself when I was your age. Unfortunately that was a time when being a nerd was not cool. Lucky for you, Bill Gates, Steve Jobs and Mark Zuckerberg have made nerdism fashionable."

"I wanted to speak to you about history and archeology. As an archeologist, I uncover the clues to the past. I piece these clues together to tell a story. Hopefully we learn something from these stories; things that let us know our position in history and how we fit in with the natural world. I'm sure that you all have heard the notion that our grandparents, long ago, were monkeys! By the way I see some of the boys fidgeting out there, your parents might say that you have more monkey blood in you than we'd like to admit! Yes, yes, I guess you could say we were 'descended from monkeys' in a manner of speaking, but that specific line was invented by people who wanted to derail the work of a very important man. Does anyone know who that man was?"

Castilia threw up her hand along with a 7th grade boy to her right. Much to her dismay, Professor Finch chose the older boy. She lowered her hand and scowled at the boy.

"Darwin," he mumbled.

"Yes, Charles Darwin, very good. At the time, no one wanted to believe that we were actually the same as all of the other animals on the planet. The Bible states that man will hold dominion over the animals. We were, as that belief goes, created in the likeness of God. That notion elevates us to our civilized status. Saying that we were monkeys upset a great deal of people and surprisingly, even after years of evidence that supports Darwin's theory, still upsets people today. The archeologist, however, has to keep an open mind. We find things buried on earth and have to often guess what they are and what they do. I can't tell you how many fossilized bones that when initially discovered were thought to be some sort of horn or bill on a giant lizard only to be reassigned as a simple leg bone after further evidence was uncovered. Archeology has a habit of making a fool out of the best of us. I like to think that is why we are so humble," he said with a sideways smile.

"My work has taken me all over the world, and I believe it is another key in the story of our relationship to nature. All cultures and religions, past and present, share many of the same ideas and beliefs. However there is one idea that is older than the rest and seems to pop up almost everywhere. From the simplest of African tribes, to Plato, to Native Americans, and even the dominate Christian religion - it is the notion that everything was created from natural elements."

Hearing the word "elements" almost made Castilia jump out of her seat. She looked around to see other reactions and noticed the the teachers and other museum adults seemed to be rolling their eyes.

Professor Finch continued, "The unusual thing about this is that time and again, through eons and eons, every culture divided the earthly elements into four categories: Earth, Wind, Fire and Water. These four elements were believed to be the origins of everything, including us…and monkeys." He paused to let this sink in.

Castilia slowly raised her hand. How cool was it that she was hearing this she thought. Professor Finch saw her hand and nodded at her. Castilia said, "What about the fifth element?"

Professor Finch's eyes widened and a wide grin slowly pushed his jowls up his face. He was not an attractive man and this grinning made him look even more like a Pug. Castilia wasn't sure if he was cute like a Pug or creepy like a man who looked liked a Pug.

"My dear," Professor Finch answered. "I've been giving this lecture for more than ten years and in all that time, not a single person has ever asked me that question. It is," he took a breath, "a sincerely fabulous question. As you may know, my life's work has been dedicated to determining the answer to that very question." He paused for a moment and looked up to the ceiling, gathering his thoughts. Castilia overheard one of their guides say softly, "Oh, here we go."

"In every culture there is good and evil." Professor Finch said with delight. "Without good there is no evil, and without evil, no good. It is the quintessential foundation on which every good story, moral, and religion is based. Yet, they are virtually the same. It is a perceptual riddle that we don't have time to discuss at present. As with the four elements, every culture also had its fifth element. It is the tie that binds everything together. It is the power that reigns over all. It is creation itself. It is the good and evil," he looked at Castilia as if to ask if that answer was sufficient.

"That doesn't make any sense, it doesn't answer anything," she said raising her left eyebrow.

"Indeed it does not. That is what makes it such a grand question. It is one that I have spent my life trying to make sense of. Just like with most things in archeology, the picture is not complete. Some say that the idea of the elements is figurative not literal; that the elements represent some relationship to God. Others say that it is simply the definition of physics. I think it is a little of both. Being a scientist, I require proof before a conclusion can be made. I have found mention of relics that are associated with the elements in a few texts, but unfortunately these relics seem to be lost. I believe, however, the relics are still in existence. These relics could hold the answer to this mystery. I hope one day to unravel it."

Castilia raised her hand again and Prof. Finch smiled grinned at her again. "Yes, young lady. Do you have another question?"

"What are the relics?" Castilia asked.

"My, we do have an inquisitive group today. I should not be surprised at such curiosity coming from a summer academic camp, should I?" Professor Finch answered. Unfortunately, he was all to used to the hordes of glassy eyed students, fidgeting and whispering through his short lecture. It was actually nice to have a few questions for a change. The adults in the class usually grumbled, and he was well aware of the derision towards his theories and research. "The writing on the relics are all very vague which is perhaps intentional as the relics may be the key to unlocking the power of the fifth element. By all accounts, the relics are rather small; capable of being easily hidden. I suspect they would be some sort of jewelry, possibly gold or silver, but more likely copper as that was the first metal to be cast, but I am not certain. They could be idols, or simple ritualistic items like bowls or cups. The fact of the matter is that we do not know." Professor Finch smiled and nodded in Castilia's general direction only to see Castilia's hand waving again high above her head.

"At that I must see you on your way. I believe you still have much to see as the Peabody itself can help you unravel many mysteries. I hope you enjoy the rest of your time here." Professor Finch smiled and graciously bowed as he left the lectern and exited through a side door. Before the door closed, he turned his head and gave Castilia another grin.

As the children filed out of the lecture hall, Professor Finch slid back into the room and asked a chaperone who that smart young lady was who had asked the questions.

"Castilia Presley is her name," the chaperone said.

"Lovely girl," he said as he turned and left the building.

CHAPTER 9

Westville

That night Castilia filled in her brothers and sister about the lecture by Professor Finch and how he lived in Westville. She had spent the rest of the day thinking about what he said; particularly the part about the relics.

"Maybe we should go visit Professor Finch and tell him what we found and show him your necklace," Castilia finished.

"Wait a second. Finch? Did you say Finch? I hope he's not related to Argus Finch," Samson said with a sneer. "Actually I would think that is impossible. This professor actually sounded smart."

"You think he is Argus's father?" Thisbe chimed in.

Argus Finch was the troublemaking bully in Samson's grade in school. Argus was the only kid in the sixth grade with a mustache. He had big everything: head, nose, neck, fists, belly, and feet. He made a habit of breeding terror wherever he went. He didn't really have any friends and didn't seem to be bothered by that fact. He was quiet and kept to himself as long as no one bothered him. No one was really sure how old he was, but rumor had it that he had been kicked out of several schools and had flunked the third and fourth grade, which would make him thirteen or fourteen years old. He stooped over when he walked so you couldn't really tell how tall he was but Samson suspected he was actually even larger that he looked. He had moved to Westville two years ago. Since that time, Argus's favorite thing to do in school was to trip or punch Samson when he least expected it. The problem was that Argus's timing was always perfect. He had the uncanny ability of performing his malicious acts when no one was looking. Almost every time the ensuing calamity ended with Samson getting reprimanded in one form or another. The one time Samson tried to confront Argus, the situation spiraled out of control until Samson was accused of bullying and was given detention for a week. After that, Samson did his best to ignore Argus. But Argus was tenacious. The only silver lining was that Argus did not participate in sports. He never showed up at parties or after school activities. He was only around during school hours and then he disappeared. This, of course, was fine by Samson.

"If that is Argus's father, then you can forget it. I'm not going anywhere near that moron or his family for any reason." Samson said in a huff.

"OK, OK, We all know how you feel about Argus. So what do you propose to do next?" Castilia said looking at Samson.

"I don't have the slightest clue," Samson crossed his arms and sat down with a "Harumph." Argus Finch always made him cross.

"Why don't we google Professor Finch? He seemed to know an awful lot about the Elements." Wylde suggested.

"Brilliant idea, brother. Why didn't I think of that?" Castilia chimed in brightly.

"Perhaps it's because you are not as smart as I am." Wylde chided with a smile.

They quickly ran to mother's computer, looked up Bartamus Finch, and found several thousand hits. Bartamus Finch had written several books on the subject of the Elements all of which were universally derided by critics and scholars alike. It seemed Professor Finch was the laughing stock of academic archeology. His views on the universal religiosity of the Elements were notoriously panned from religious centers to conspiracy theorists.

After reading some of the articles and reviews Castilia said, "Hum... maybe we should look elsewhere for some information. This guy seems like a nut."

"I told you," Samson retorted with glee. "Any father of Argus has got to be crazy."

"So now what do we do?" Thisbe asked.

"Maybe we should go down to the Historical Society and look up that map of Fox Hollow. Maybe that will lead to something," Wylde suggested.

"That's a good idea, Wylde. I don't see that we have any other options at this point," Castilia said thoughtfully. "We can ride our bikes up there Saturday morning."

The rest of the camp week continued uneventfully. Samson finally got into a plane on Friday and was the only one in the group that was allowed to take the controls. He had worked harder that week than at any time during school. He learned what all of the instruments, dials and monitors did and how they worked. He knew all of the terminology, and even did extra research after camp. Mom and Dad were amazed. They said he would be a straight "A" student if he applied himself like that in school. Samson replied that school was three quarters of a year, not a week, and learning to fly was cool, unlike anything he ever learned in school. It was hard work doing all that studying. Besides, he was exhausted.

Saturday morning came and the four siblings rode their bikes the back way to town down the less traveled dirt roads. It had been hot and dry for a couple of weeks so each time a car did pass them they all got a face full of dust. By the time they got to the paved road coming into town they looked like they had farmed the dust bowl. Castilia knew she should have worn a hat. Now her hair was all dusty. The stupid bike helmet always messed her hair up too. She was definitely going to need a shower when she got back. No one else seemed to be bothered. Being dirty actually made Wylde look more normal.

Westville Road ran right through the half mile long metropolis of downtown Westville. The road was lined with a couple of blocks of local businesses. There was a pharmacy, a grocery store, a coffee shop, a diner, a dry cleaner and a hardware store to name a few. The two blocks of the commercial district were quaint wood clapboard and brick storefronts with second story apartments. The sidewalks were a brick and the overall feel was very typically New England. It seemed nothing had changed on the street for a century except for electric light, asphalt paving and then eventually plastic or neon signage.

At the center of downtown on the East side of the street sat the Westville Town Hall. It was a grand Greek Revival brick building complete with ionic columns that had been built in 1874 on the spot of the old town hall which had burned to the ground after a lighting strike hit the wooden structure. The Town Hall stoically faced Fenimore Park, which is more commonly known as the Westville Green or simply, The Green. The Green was the center of Westville and was home to the Town pavilion, which was the site of the annual Memorial Day Fair as well as the Autumn Harvest Festival. The Green also provided a venue for summer concerts and picnics. It was a nice place to sit and pass time reading a good book in the shade of a large Elm tree, or playing Frisbee on the open lawn.

The Green is flanked by Chapel Street and Church Street, both running west from the main road. True to their names, the roads were the home to two Westville churches, which also faced the Green. On the North side, The Presbyterian Church was a white clapboard structure with a single center spire and the tallest structure in Westville. The second tallest structure was on the opposite side of the green and home to the Second True Congregation of Christ. It was a lovely stone gothic church that had inspired to have two lofty towers of which only one was fully constructed, albeit without its leaded spire. The plans for the original spire caused a firestorm that nearly tore the town apart in the early 1800s. The Presbyterian Church, which had proudly ruled the Westville skyline for a century by the time the new stone church was proposed, was up in arms at the prospect of having their beloved spire usurped by some new upstart. The powerful citizens and members of the Presbyterian Church managed to "persuade" the new church to propose a more humble house for God. It was later said that the new pastor of the Second Congregation and one or more of his more prominent member's wives may have had inappropriate confessionals of which the Presbyterians sought to expose if the tower met its overreaching potential. Needless to say, the funds for the exuberant tower did not ultimately materialize and it still stands second fiddle today.

Six beautiful houses flanked the churches to fill in the street-scape around the park. They were all very elegant and important houses built by the oldest and most prestigious families of Westville, each one bigger and more opulent than the next.

The western end of the Green was the location of the Westville Historical Society, which is the most opulent home in the town. It is a grand Victorian mansion with three levels, a beautiful slate roof, and a large front porch facing the green. It was built by the Vandermost Family in the early 1800s. The family, with all its prominence and wealth, soon found itself without an heir. At the death of the last Hubert Hamilton Vandermost in 1893, the house was donated to the town to be used as the mayoral mansion. It had been the mayoral mansion for over seventy years when it was the subject in a wonderful scandal. Mayor Everton Fitzgerald, who presided over Westville from 1950 to 1966 and was a prominent local businessman, decided that his virtuous civil duty was worth a good bit more than he was actually being paid by the Town of Westville. Over his 16 year tenure, he was able to extort several million dollars through bogus Town building projects and contracts. Just after winning his fifth consecutive term as Mayor he promptly disappeared from town with the town treasurer, Ms. Josephine Martuchio, who was suspected to be his mistress. His disappearance narrowly preceded a newspaper expose outlining his alleged corruption. It was only after their disappearance that it was discovered that the Town was virtually bankrupt and the Mayor had been stealing the money since he first got into office. The Mayor was found down in Florida years later, a homeless vagabond claiming that

JoJo set him up and took all of his money. He was sent to an asylum. Josephine was never seen or heard from again. A picture of the couple hangs in the Historical Society as a reminder to future generations of municipal malfeasance. Dad was on the Board of the Historical Society and would constantly bring up the story whenever one of them asked for money. Apparently he sat opposite the picture at every meeting.

After the scandal, the mayoral mansion was the first building to be sold off to raise much needed capital. A consortium of local businesses and citizens bought the house and created the Westville Historical Society Trust. Mayoral term limits were also soon voted into the town charter.

Samson, Castilia, Thisbe and Wylde made their way through town to The Green where there was a bike stand near the pavilion. It was another hot day and the shade of The Green's large Elm and Oak trees was a welcome respite from the blazing sun. They parked and locked their bikes and took a moment to rest in the shade with a light snack Thisbe had prepared. Samson ran down the street to the Thrifty Mart to get everyone a cool drink. He ran out of the park and down the brick sidewalk on Main Street when he was suddenly hit in the stomach by something very large that immediately took his breath away, and he fell to the ground, also skinning his knee. He was seeing stars and couldn't catch his breath. His eyes were watering as he raised his head to see what hit him and that is when he heard a repulsively familiar voice.

"Ha ha. Thanks Presley, I've missed that. Nothing like an unexpected surprise to turn your whole day around. And I thought it was just going to be another boring day."

Still gasping for air, Samson was able to look around to see the towering silhouette of the person standing over him. Amazingly, there was not a single other person on the street.

CHAPTER 10

Argus Finch

As soon as Samson left the park, Castilia, of course, changed her mind. She wanted a Root Beer instead of a Ginger Ale so she took off after Samson to change her order. Once she crossed the street and rounded the corner to the main street, she could see Samson laid out on the sidewalk with a large figure standing over him. She raced toward him to see what was going on.

"Get away from my brother, Argus!" Castilia yelled as she approached. Argus Finch jerked his big head in her direction and gave a contented smile.

"I'm done with him," he said with a smirk raising one side of his mustachioed lip which made him look even more devious. "You can have him." And he nonchalantly lumbered away.

Samson had managed to pull himself up to one knee and was finally catching his breath. The anxiety he felt from not breathing was now being replaced by full-throttled anger. He was definitely seeing red. Sometimes Samson's anger would consume him and take over every thought in his head. It was the famous

Presley temper, something the Presleys had struggled with for generations. His father had taught him not to react to it but to pause and take ten breaths before doing anything. Everyone in the family knew to let him get control before engaging him again. Samson felt incredibly hot, like he was melting. This time felt different. He didn't know if he could make this pass.

"Oh my God, are you OK?" Castilia said in a low voice and reached out to help her brother up.

"OUCH!!!" she screamed, holding her hand back in pain, "what the heck?"

Samson felt like he was close to exploding when a coolness filled his chest and spread across his body, pushing the anger aside. It was like someone was pouring ice cold water over his body. He was able to compose himself slightly and stand up. His head was clearing like the sun burning off the morning fog. He looked around and saw his sister holding her hand and looking at him as if he were a ghost. Her expression changed to surprise as her eyes moved to his chest.

"It's glowing again" she said in awe.

Samson looked down to see the amulet slowly dimming. It has burned a hole in his shirt and was still smoldering.

Castilia slowly reached out to Samson and quickly touched his arm as if testing for something. "You were burning hot. I think I blistered my hand when I tried to help you up. And you were red like you were really sunburned. But now you seem normal. Are you OK?" she said putting her hand up to his face like her mother did when they were sick.

"I'm fine, I think," Samson said coming out of his daze and actually accessing his body and looking around. He fingered the hole in his shirt and checked his chest behind the amulet, but it was as smooth and normal as ever. His only visible injury was the blood stain on his shin from his skinned knee which didn't really hurt and had already stopped bleeding "Are you OK? You look like you are hurt. Let me see your hand."

Castilia held out the hand she had been cradling in her armpit. Samson held her hand up as tenderly as he could to get a better look. "It's really red, looks like a sunburn. Let's go to the store and get some ice."

Samson led his sister to the convenience store and bought a couple of large drinks and also got a large cup of ice which Castilia was easily able to stuff her hand into. They then slowly walked back to the park sipping on Ginger Ale and Root Beer, still in shock.

Seeing his brother and sister appear around the corner, Wylde impatiently yelled, "Hey! Oh there you are… No-no-no… take your time. Thiz and I are only wallowing in puddles of our own sweat." He said sarcastically. "How were the video games in the air conditioned…" He continued, but was cut off by Thisbe.

"Whoa! What happened?" She said as she jumped up and ran to her dazed siblings. She helped them both down to the blanket they had laid out under a large oak and promptly fed them snacks and fruit as Castilia filled them in. By the time she had finished, Thisbe had surveyed them both and the damage seemed to be minimal. She took out some water and began washing Samson's wounded knee. For so much blood there didn't even seem to be a cut.

"Why does he do that?" Thisbe said to Samson as she was putting things away.

"What? Who do what?" In all that had happened Samson had almost forgotten that Argus had jumped out of nowhere and punched him in the stomach for no reason.

"Why does Argus always hit you?" she clarified, her voice calm and concerned.

"Oh…Well, he came to Westville a couple of years ago when I was in fourth grade. He was big and ugly and new. At recess one day a group of us got rollin' on some 'your mama' jokes. I was showing off in front of Michael and Jake and turned the focus on Argus. They were real good and I had everyone laughing pretty hard. Argus turned red and looked like he was going to cry, which just made me keep going. He took everything I threw at him and never dropped a tear but just turned around and walked away. I found out later that his mom died or something a few years ago. As soon as I found out, I went up to him at the end of recess and tried to apologize to him when no one was looking because I was embarrassed about being such a jerk, but he just decked me. We were the last two outside and he left me there rolling around on the ground. No one saw what happened and I was late getting back to class so I got in trouble. When Ms. Coulter sent me to the office, it was the first time I saw him smile. I couldn't rat him out at that point because of what I did to him, so I just took my lumps and let it go, and figured we were even. Little did I know that he was just getting started. He's been doing it ever since. It's almost like he plans his day around how he can get away with hurting or embarrassing me. It's not like he does it to impress anyone or make anyone laugh, it's solely for my benefit. After that year, he sort of branched out and started bullying some of my friends too. We think he enjoys it now and he can't stop. He sort of has a reputation now as a badass. No one really bothers him because everyone is scared of him. I think I created a monster."

"That's a pretty bad thing you did but I'm not sure you deserve to get punished for two years," Thisbe said thoughtfully. She had cleared the picnic at this point and put on her backpack. "Let's go over to the Historical Society."

They gathered their things and threw away their trash and traversed the park to the Historical Society. They walked up the wooden steps to the porch and entered the front door.

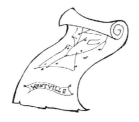

CHAPTER 11

Historical Society

"Excuse me, children," said Ms. Cornblatt, the volunteer greeter as the kids came up the stairs and opened the door to the Historical Society, " you can't come in here like that."

Samson looked at her causiously, "Why not?"

"Because you are filthy. Look at you, your shirt's ripped, and you're all dirty as dogs. Is that blood on your leg young man?" She continued, spreading her arms out to shoo them back out of the building. "You'll have to come back another day. Where are your parents?"

Samson, Castilia and Wylde looked around at each other and they were, indeed, filthy. Wylde in particular seemed to have covered himself from head to foot with dirt. The dusty sweaty ride into town, along with the beat down made them look like street orphans. All except for Thisbe, who was remarkably clean. Ms. Cornblatt did not even seem to be addressing her at all, like she just happened to enter the building at the same time as these urchins but was not with them. Ms. Cornblatt continued to corral the three miscreants outside, leaving Thisbe to continue into the Historical Society museum and library.

Thisbe walked breezily through the foyer entrance and under the stairs to the Historical Society Library where she found the librarian sitting behind the entry desk. She had grey hair tied into a bun, just as you would expect a librarian to look. She was wearing a cardigan sweater despite the heat outside, and had a pair of reading glasses resting on the tip of her nose. The book she was reading had a worn leather cover and yellow pages.

"Excuse me, Ma'am," Thisbe said softly. This startled the woman, who hadn't heard her approach.

"Oh, my goodness dear, you startled me. What can I do for you this morning?" the librarian asked.

"Umm.. I wanted to look at some old maps of Westville," Thisbe hesitantly said. She was used to Samson and Castilia taking the lead in things like this. She vary rarely had to ask for anything or really talk to anyone. This was something she wasn't very used to. Not that she particularly minded too much, but the newness of it was weird and a bit scary.

"We have many maps of Westville, was there something in particular you were looking for?" the librarian inquired.

"Um.. yes. I live over on Fox Hollow Farm and wanted to see what maps you had of that. My Mom said there was an old Indian burial ground on the property." Thisbe explained. The librarian stepped back and looked her up and down for a moment.

"My goodness, you must be one of the Presley kids. I should have known with your beautiful blond hair and pretty blue eyes. It's been so long since I've seen any of you. Which one are you?"

"Thisbe," Thisbe said, " the third one."

67

"It is so nice to meet you Thisbe. My name is Mrs. Grumman and I grew up in your house." She said smiling down at Thisbe. She continued, "I know all about Fox Hollow - it has a grand history. I expected I'd see one of you in here before long. I'm sure you've heard all the stories about the house being haunted, right?"

"Haunted?" Thisbe shivered and looked back at Mrs. Grumman with wide eyes. "Actually, no. Only that my mom said that there was an Indian burial ground on the farm. My brothers and sister came here with me today to see if we could find out anything because we found…" Thisbe almost told her about the temple but she decided to change her story, "some arrow heads and Mom told us Ms. Jenkins said there was an Indian burial ground."

"I see. Where are the others?" Mrs. Grumman said looking around.

"They got thrown outside for being too dirty by the lady at the front." Thisbe replied with a worried look on her face, as if that information was going to send her out onto the porch as well.

"Well, we can't have dirty hands messing up all of our important artifacts, now can we? Let's see if I can help you find what you are looking for," Ms. Grumman said as she began to walk toward the book stacks behind her desk and nodded at Thisbe to follow. "You came to the right place. Fox Hollow has a long and quite mysterious past."

"If I remember correctly, the farm was one of the first in the town. It was, in fact, here before the town was incorporated. It was started by an English family of Transcendentalists. They grew corn and potatoes early on and had chickens, cows and goats which was fairly typical for the time. The house now standing on the property was not the original homestead but dates from around 1820 I believe. We can look that up if you are interested." She was walking toward a large horizontal cabinet with wide thin drawers. The drawers had a placard in the center which she ran her finger down until she came to the fifth drawer and opened it. She rifled through a few sheets of large yellow paper until she found what she was looking for and pulled out a large map and placed it on the top of the cabinet. "Here we are" she said, smoothing out the old parchment map and pointing to an area in the center. The map was dated 1943. "Fox Hollow was much larger back then as you can see here. I believe the farm was owned by the Martuchio family at that point. There were only a few dirt horse and carriage roads back then that led to the old foundry up to the north in the valley and the mill by the pond near your house. Most of the area's industry was making charcoal. The abundance of nice hardwood made this a perfect area for that occupation. This map shows the extent of the property and…here it is," she said pointing at a circle near the house, "the Indian burial ground. You can see the annotation is very vague, not much importance was put on anything Native American back then. It's actually quite odd that the burial ground is even mentioned on this map. It seems to be about half way between your house to the pond."

"Can I get a copy of this map to show my Mom?" Thisbe asked

"Of course dear," Ms. Grumman said, picking up the map and moving back toward her desk. "But I have to tell you, this Indian burial ground is the least fascinating thing about the property. When I was young we looked for this thing for years but never found any evidence of it anywhere. The best we could tell it should have been around the location of the hill along the path to the pond. We never so much as found a single arrowhead in that location. My brothers must have dug up most of that hill looking for anything having to do with Native Americans. We all figured it must have been some mistake on the map, but it does make for a good story."

"You said the house was haunted?" Thisbe asked as she followed the librarian through the bookcases.

"Oh, yes. That is the rumor." She said as she turned and smiled at Thisbe. "However, we always found the house to be more magical than haunted. Strange and wonderful things always happened in the house, nothing ever scary or spooky," she continued with a wink. They made it back to the desk and Mrs. Grumman operated the copy machine to make a copy of the map for Thisbe. " To me, the house had a personality all its own, it seemed to like some people and dislike others. It also seemed to actively protect everyone in the house." Ms. Grumman handed Thisbe the map as two other people entered the library.

"If you really want to learn about the house, you should visit my mother who lived there for over 60 years and sold the house to your parents. She lives with me now over on Farrell Road. She would love the opportunity to entertain some guests and tell you what she knows. Her name is Mrs. Goodwyn and the number is 288. Come by anytime if you like. I'll give her a call and let her know you will drop by."

"I'd like that very much. Thank you for your help and the copy of the map." Thisbe said as Ms. Grumman headed toward the newcomers and gave her a parting wave. Thisbe grabbed a pencil at the desk and wrote 'Godwin 288 Feral' on the corner of her copy of the map and walked out of the library in search of the others. She found them all despondent and dirty, sitting just outside on the front steps of the building. They all jumped up when she come out of the door, curious to see what she found. Thisbe showed them the map and told them about Mrs. Grumman and her mother Ms. Goodwyn.

"That's the lady Mom told us about in the story," Samson confirmed. " We should definitely go see her."

"She's got to be really old," Thisbe said, "Ms. Grumman, the librarian, was an old lady with gray hair and Mrs. Goodwyn is her mother. I wonder if she remembers anything."

"Thisbe, not every old person is like Grandma Seward was." Castilia scolded.

"But Grandma Seward kept on calling me Daisy," Thisbe recalled, "that's Mom's name." The thought of her great grandmother before she died always made her upset.

"Mom told you she was sick and she didn't mean it. Anyway, I'm sure the librarian wouldn't have invited us over if Mrs. Goodwyn had lost it," Castilia said, "We can't go over there now. We're apparently too dirty to do anything. Let's go home, clean up and get some lunch. Then we can bike over to Farrell Road and see if she is there."

CHAPTER 12

Mrs. Goodwyn

That afternoon they again mounted their bikes and made the trek to town. This time, however, they took the main roads to keep themselves from getting too dirty. Farrell Road was a twisty hilly road just like all the others in Westville, however it was close to town and tended to be less hilly and twisty than some. Trees lined the street and tried to keep as much sun off the pavement as possible, but shards of light stubbornly rifled through the foliage. The good thing about Farrell Road, if there was a good thing, was that it consisted of smaller houses on smaller lots with a sidewalk on both sides of the street so they knew that the house would not take too long to find. 288 Farrell Road unfortunately seemed to be at the highest point on the blasted street, 288 houses away from town. As they continued down the street into the 100s the sidewalk became more broken and heaved. They moved onto the street which became shaded as the trees were more successful at blocking the sunlight. The last stretch of road up to 288 seemed to be almost vertical as they all huffed and puffed up the hill. At the top they passed 280 and started to descend to their destination but as they gathered speed down the hill the numbered mail boxes 290, 292, 294 flew past them. Castilia slammed on her brakes. "STTTOOOPP!!!!! WE MISSED IT!" She yelled in her loudest voice. The rest of the group skidded to a halt and looked back at her and up the hill they just descended with consternation.

"WHAT?!!! How did we do that?," Samson said in frustration as he had made it further down the hill than anyone and had the farthest to get back up the hill. "Stupid hill," he said as he started back up the hill. 300, 298, 296...

They finally made it back to the top and stopped in front of 2 dirty old stone pillars through which a slightly overgrown dirt driveway wound further up the hill. On the right of the pillars was a faded white mailbox with 280 in faded black numbers written on it but the 0 was half as tall as the eight.

"This is it," Castilia said breathlessly

"No it's not!," Samson said tired and frustrated, "It's 280, stupid. We've got to go back down the hill again." He turned his bike around to head down the hill again in disgust.

"It is 288 mushbrain," Castilia retorted, "the top of the last eight fell off. See." She said pointing at the smaller 0 beside the eight. After a little grumbling and half-hearted arguing Samson conceded the point to his sister. To the left and right, 286 and 290 stood close by and were split level ranch houses that were built in the 60s and clearly a newer addition to the street. Their lawns and mailboxes had been given much more attention recently making 288 look a little careworn. The drive led up to a backlot so the house could not be seen from the street. They looked up the steep driveway and decided to bag the bikes at the road and hike the rest of the way up. They parked their bikes neatly to the side of the driveway beside the left pillar so they were out of the way. They took off their helmets and inspected themselves after the long ride. Samson, Castilia and Thisbe looked fairly presentable. Wylde was tinkering with his bike and had his back to his brother and sisters as he took off his helmet and placed it on his handlebars. He turned around ready to go to the house at which time Castilia looked sideways at Wylde.

"What happened to you?" she said to him.

"What?" he answered as he looked at his sister then inspected himself. Samson started laughing heartily. Wylde looked just as dusty and sweaty as he did this morning.

"Good gracious. If I hadn't actually seen you washing up, I would swear you did nothing of the sort. You really are a dirt magnet. Jeesh...There's nothing we can do about it now. Try not to touch anything if we get inside." Castilia said as she turned and ventured up the drive as it headed further up the hill. The driveway twisted up to a small Victorian farmhouse neatly perched between two massive oak trees. It was old, dark and dusty. The white paint was fading and pealing off of its surface. Several of the dark shutters hung roughshod from one broken hinge. The lawn was in need of mowing and had patches of dirt from skunks digging grubs.

Castilia turned to Wylde once they all took in the view of the house and said, "remember what I said about not touching anything? Perhaps that doesn't really matter." She then proceeded to walk up the weed strewn walk and up the creaky wooden steps to the front door. Everyone followed. Thisbe rang the bell and it coughed like it hadn't been rung in years. They could see the flicker of a television from deep inside the house from the dusty sidelites beside the door. A shadow passed in front of the flickering light in response to the ringing of the bell. Someone was definitely in the house though it was hard to tell through the dirty glass. Impatient, Samson rang the bell again. They could see the silhouette of a person slowly making her way to the front door.

"This is taking forever." Samson mumbled under his breath.

"Hush," Castilia chastised, "she's got to be over 90 years old. You should move so fast at that age."

After a few more moments and several more deep sighs by Samson, someone came up to the door. It took several seconds of fiddling with the various locks and latches on the door. When the door finally but slowly opened, it gave out a loud soulful groan and screech. Through the crack of the door a raspy whisper of a voice said, "Can I help you?"

Thisbe took the lead, "Hi, I'm Thisbe. Your daughter said we could come see you and ask you some questions."

Castilia jumped in to clarify a bit, "Questions about our house, Fox Hollow Farm."

The door slowly creaked opened and the light spilled into the opening to reveal the oldest woman any of them had ever seen. She was as wrinkly as an elephant and her long thin gray hair was pulled back into an unkempt bun with long wispy stands of hair flowing across her face. Her eyes seems slightly hazy, like a frosty windshield, and she was wearing only what could be described as a floral tablecloth that was masquerading as a house dress. Thisbe, slowly, almost imperceptibly, moved behind Samson. They were all amazed that the old woman was actually moving much less breathing. As the light hit the old woman's face she squinted her eyes against the glare, making her face look even more wrinkly than it seemed before. After a moment she was able to look upon her visitors and she gave a wide yellow toothed smile and seemed to straighten herself a little.

"Bless me, you finally came...I've been expecting you. Come in, come in." she said in a dusty old voice as she opened the door wider and seemed to move a little quicker. "Please, let's sit in the parlor, or what my daughter likes to call the family room, straight ahead down the hall. Would you like some chocolate milk? Perhaps some cookies?"

They all paused a moment looking incredulously at the old woman standing in the doorway.

"Cookies would be nice," Thisbe said uncharacteristically and walked past the door into the house. The others looked at one another in sudden amazement.

"I'll have some chocolate milk," Wylde said as he followed his sister.

"Me too," Samson and Castilia both chorused and walked inside as the old woman closed the door behind them.

The house was dim and dusty as all of the shades were drawn. A console TV was blaring at almost full volume on some daytime talk show where people were fighting and calling each other names that were continually bleeped out loudly every other second.

"It's awful, I know, but sometimes I get bored and there really isn't anything on TV in the middle of the day. Unfortunately some days my eyes are so bad it makes it too hard to read," Mrs. Goodwyn said as she finally shuffled into the parlor and turned off the TV. "Please have a seat while I get the refreshments and snacks. Young lady," she said to Thisbe, "would you mind giving me a hand in the kitchen?"

"I'd be happy to," Thisbe said with a smile.

"And could you ask your strapping brothers to open up the drapes and let some light into this room so we may speak together with some civility?" she said as she headed to the kitchen.

"Samson and Wylde..." Thisbe waved her hand toward the curtains and disappeared out of the room to find their host.

Samson and Wylde quickly opened up the drapes to relieve the room of some of its creepiness. It was a small room with a long sofa with what looked like a pattern of flowers and birds on the fabric, however, it was very faded and could have been almost anything. The sofa had several homemade knit pillows that were inscribed with banal sayings like "Home is where the Heart is" and "the Queen rules this castle". A coffee table littered with gossip magazines was in front of the sofa and two other chairs faced the wall where the giant wooden TV console now sat silent and dark. Samson and Wylde stared curiously at this odd antique. On the tops of the sofa and chairs lay slightly yellowed lacy doilies. The other walls hung varied framed pictures of generations of children, grandchildren and great grandchildren.

Mrs. Goodwyn slowly returned with Thisbe behind her carrying a tray of goodies. She shuffled to the coffee table and quickly made a space for Thisbe to place the tray, which she did. "Please help yourself," Mrs. Goodwyn waved her hand over the tray, "I must excuse myself for just a moment to make myself more presentable. I hope you understand, I have not received visitors for quite some time and I am desperately out of practice." With that she slowly made her way out of the room and turned down another hall and disappeared.

"These cookies are awesome," Wylde said through a mouthful of crumbs. The tray included four tall glasses of chocolate milk and several varieties of homemade cookies and treats. As none of the Presley clan was apt to turn down a sweet of any kind they all indulged themselves with the milk and cookies and politely waited for their guest to return.

After a while, they heard footsteps emanating from the hall Mrs. Goodwyn retreated and they anxiously stared at the opening as the noise grew louder. A completely different woman, or so it seemed, appeared from the hall off of the foyer. She was much taller and several decades younger than the old woman that had let them in the house. She was wearing a nice light blue dress with a white cardigan sweater and had a pair of horn rimmed glasses perched upon her angular nose. Her hair seemed fuller but was just as gray and her wrinkles were oh so much more diminished. She smiled at her visitors and smoothed her dress as she walked into the Parlor.

"I do hope I did not keep you waiting too long." she said pleasantly. "I'm Mrs. Goodwyn, I'm pleased to make your acquaintance." Her voice was much less dusty and old now and seem invigorated.

Castilia, remembering her manners as she had read in the Emily Post etiquette books said, "It was no bother at all, I hope you will forgive us for barging in on you so. I'm Castilia Presley," Castilia stood up and introduced herself, "and this is my sister Thisbe and brothers Samson and Wylde," she said as she pointed to her sister and brothers in turn. They nodded to their host as they were being introduced. 'Your daughter said we should come to see you. I guess you got her message."

Mrs. Goodwyn smiled down at Castilia, seemingly impressed by her tact. "Actually, no. My daughter did not warn me of your visit I am disappointed to say."

"But you said you were expecting us," Castilia continued curiously.

Mrs. Goodwyn made her way around the room to the open easy chair. "I've been expecting you for some time, my friends. I figured you would have questions at some point." She slowly sat in the chair and smoothed her skirt once she was settled.

Everyone stared at the old lady in wonder. She seemed like some sort of prophet. It was very unsettling, but Castilia pressed on. "How were you expecting us?"

"I'm sure you've found something at Fox Hollow that seems very unlikely, perhaps magical and you've come to me to see if I know anything about it. Well, clearly I do know some things but unfortunately I do not know enough." She said with a smile which made her face light up. Her wrinkles, again, seemed to recede.

"Wow, that is so creepy," Samson said impetuously.

"Samson!" Castilia scolded.

"Sorry," he stammered, redfaced. "What I meant was that you seem to know stuff about us that we haven't told anyone." He explained.

"Indeed I do," Mrs. Goodwyn began, " I've known about this moment for quite a while actually. I was beginning to think that I was not going to live to see it, but here you are and amazingly here I am too."

"So you know about the temple?" Thisbe said meekly, looking around as if to keep anyone else from hearing.

"Temple?", Mrs. Goodwyn said, "I don't know anything about a temple but perhaps you found the Chamber of Transition, or at least that's how I've come to know it. It is the place that inhabits the property. It is neither here nor there. It is found only when it needs to be found. It is not a religious place as you are not praying to anyone, nor is it the earthly home of some deity. It is a place in which your full potential can be known."

"Potential?... I don't really understand anything that you said. What does that mean?" Wylde asked.

"I guess I should explain to you my experiences at Fox Hollow and how those experiences lead me to leave the property to your parents... and in turn to you," Mrs. Goodwyn answered. She looked around at everyone and adjusted herself in her chair until she was looking rather comfortable.

"I've thought about that property more than anyone in their right mind should have but I guess that's the point, isn't it? My husband and I always thought we were fated to live on Fox Hollow farm but came to know over the years that we were there for a different reason. We did not choose the farm but the farm chose us. We were able to live in that place and raise a family while waiting for the rightful owners. But it was not a simple waiting game - things were revealed to us so that we would be able to help guide the next generation. So we were simply chosen as the stewards of the property to keep Fox Hollow until Time and Fate reconciled themselves to relinquish it to the next coming. Now, of course, that is probably very vague and confusing to you, but that's the way discovery goes, isn't it? I do know when your mother showed up that day that it was incredibly clear that she should have the property; it was predestined.

I knew her the moment I saw her just as I knew you when you came to my door. However, I am only able to interpret what I know of your situation because there is some knowledge in me that I am only able to know when asked of it. This knowledge I have learned over decades of living on the property as a peripheral observer. Unfortunately, I do not know the relevance of this knowledge until its substance is revealed. The only reason I know these things are important is because I am still here to pass it on to you. I feel like a reservoir that needs to be tapped. I will have to wait here in this earthly realm watching horrible daytime TV until that reservoir is depleted. Thus is my blessing and my curse."

"How did you know us when we came to your door?" Samson asked.

"I do not see very well but I know the sun when it rises in the sky, as does anyone else. This is how I knew you were here to talk to me about Fox Hollow," Mrs. Goodwyn smiled and blinked her frosted eyes.

"So what does that mean regarding the Temple or chamber we found." asked Castilia as if unconcerned with the absurdity of it all. "If you do know about the Temple what can you tell us about it?"

"The chamber will always be a safe place for you. It is a place for you to learn and grow. It is a place for you to practice and develop." she answered.

"But Samson fell in and almost got very hurt there, how could it be safe?" Castilia argued.

"Discovery is aways a dangerous prospect, but as you learn more, the unknown seems less mysterious," she said.

"Well, more importantly, I ruined my shoes and pants twice and got in trouble for it both times," Castilia said seriously, " and that doesn't seem like a nurturing place to me."

"Life is full of hard lessons. Sometimes lessons are not learned the first, second or even third times but the lessons continue to be taught all the same."

"Haha, I think she's calling you stupid, Castilia," Wylde pointed out, "that's a new one."

"Stupidity is the act of willful disregard of the obvious." Mrs. Goodwyn calmly stated but chuckled nonetheless.

"Now you really are sounding like a creepy oracle", Samson stated giggling. They all burst out laughing and the seriousness of the situation evaporated.

"Goodness me, you are right! It seems we all need a little loosening up. Perhaps another round of chocolate milk will do the trick." Mrs. Goodwyn said as she rose and reached for the tray. Thisbe quickly intervened and took the tray back into the kitchen for more refreshments.

After the second round of chocolate milk, Mrs. Goodwyn began to excuse herself.

"I've deeply enjoyed our visit and conversation but as you can see I am an old lady and I may have exhausted myself quite fully. I'm going to have to excuse myself to rest for a while," Mrs. Goodwyn said reluctantly. At this point in the day she had lost a lot of the glow she gained during their visit and was clearly fading.

"We are sorry we stayed so long," Thisbe said gathering up the remaining dishes and heading to the kitchen.

"Leave that please, child. My daughter will happily clean up after our visit..." She paused and looked around at the disarray, "well, maybe not happily, but she will clean up nonetheless." She said with a smile and a tired chuckle.

"Can we call on you again?" Castilia asked. "There is still a lot we would like to speak with you about."

"Of course, dear. Perhaps it would be better if you were to call first and let me know when you will come by." Mrs. Goodwyn gave them her telephone number and graciously thanked them for coming by. It was the most excitement she had had in as long as she could remember. She showed the kids to the door and then drew the drapes and curtains to veil the house in darkness again and headed to her bed for a much needed rest.

Once outside Castilia lamented, "I like her, but we need to get our act together so we can get some answers. She clearly knows things that will help us figure this whole thing out." They all donned their helmets and mounted their bikes to ride home. As they turned down the street and headed towards Fox Hollow, a black sedan with tinted window pulled away from the curb and did a U-turn to follow the bikers down the street. The car passed them as they left the street and turned down the dirt shortcut toward Hwy 153 that led to their house. As they completed the ride and turned into their driveway, that same tinted sedan drove slowly by and then sped off down the road.

The next few days were uneventful as the kids began to formulate a list of questions to ask Mrs. Goodwyn. Most of the discussions revolved around whether they should reveal Samson's necklace and the things it had done. Thisbe and Wylde were convinced they could trust Mrs. Goodwyn, but Castilia and Samson were not so sure. They wanted to keep that information to themselves for a while. The two older kids were still a bit freaked out by what had happened with the amulet on the sidewalk after the encounter with Argus.

CHAPTER 13

Two Invitations

On Tuesday, Samson, Castilia and Wylde visited the Town Center while their mother did some grocery shopping. Thisbe was again at Gymnastics practice. It was another hot summer day, with a wide expansive blue sky without a single cloud spoiling the blueness. The boys began to head to the Thrift Store to play some video games in the air conditioning while Castilia noticed Dr. Lovejoy decked out all in white in front of the pharmacy across the street. He was talking to a small group of old ladies and was making wild gestures with his arms all the while sporting his trademark smile. The ladies were enraptured. Castilia convinced her brothers to come check him out for a minute.

As they approached, they heard Dr. Lovejoy's melodic voice ringing out on the sidewalk, "it's blue because it works so well with the green below." he finished waving his hand above his head. The ladies laughed as he saw Castilia and the boys approaching. He turned his attention toward the children, "Ahh, Miss Presley. It's so nice to see you again." he said with an extra large grin and giving her a wave. All of the old ladies turned to look at the blond youngsters joining their group and a shadow of disappointment washed their faces. They knew this gathering was ruined. They began to regain their sense of purpose and meander off to whatever task they had come to town to accomplish before Dr. Lovejoy stole their attention. As the crowd dispersed and Dr. Lovejoy made his way toward the Presleys, one of the ladies got under foot and jostled the papers the Reverend was carrying, spilling a few to the pavement. "Oh my goodness!" Lovejoy stammered as Samson quickly bent down to retrieve them. Most of the papers looked like hymnal sheet music, which one would expect, however one paper particularly caught Samson's eye. It had cryptic symbols that looked somewhat familiar. While he was gathering the papers, his necklace fell out of his neckline and hung over his shirt. As he stood, Dr. Lovejoy quickly relieved Samson of the papers and tucked them under his arm. He seemed a little flustered, but quickly regained his composure.

"Thank you so much, young man. May I assume I am in the presence of this fair young lady's brothers?" he began, and Wylde and Samson slowly nodded as he quickly continued. "The blond hair and blue eyes gives you away I'm afraid. You are just as fair as your lovely sister. I'm Dr. Leroy Lovejoy. It's a pleasure to make your acquaintance," he said with his trademark toothy smile extending his hand in greetings.

Samson took his hand and received a vigorous handshaking and nod. "You must be Samson, the oldest of the Presley crew and stalwart leader of the motley band as I've heard it told." Turning his attention to Wylde, he once again firmly gripped the young boy's hand and gave it a vigorous shake, "and you must be Wylde, the last of the line, the soft spoken but fierce protector of the group." Both Samson and Wylde were taken aback by this strange man's large personality.

"How do you know us?" Wylde said suspiciously.

"I wouldn't be very much of a preacher if didn't know a thing or two about the people in my community, now would I? I'm sure you are aware of how much information is shared here and there. Haven't you ever wondered how your parents always know you've been in trouble almost before you do?" Dr. Lovejoy questioned.

This, of course, was common knowledge, but to Wylde it was a bombshell. He never put it together. He just always thought his parents were clairvoyant. Never before had an adult shared some of their secrets with him. This person could be useful, he thought to himself.

"And what are you young people doing gallivanting around on a fine day like today, may I ask?"

"Nothing much," Castilia answered, "we were headed to the Thrifty Mart to play some video games when we saw you over here pontificating, so I thought I'd bring Samson and Wylde over to meet you." Castilia had just learned the word pontificate and was almost ecstatic that she had managed to use it in a sentence.

"Pontificating? My that is a big word for such a small lady, but I guess you are correct. I was pontificating." he said with a huge laugh. "That is my job after all, and speaking of my job, I must excuse myself to get ready for my next vociferous homily." Taking his leave he once again gave a monstrous smile and an exuberant shake of everyone's hand, ending with Samson. Just as he was leaving, his eye caught the dull glimmer at Samson's neck and he stopped suddenly. "My, that is a fabulous pendant you have there," he said motioning to the necklace at Samson's neck.

"Oh," Samson said looking down and pushing the medallion back under his shirt, "Thank you, it was a present from my Grandfather."

"Cherish the simple gifts of love." Dr. Lovejoy said as he walked away.

"See," Castilia said to her brothers. "Isn't he a trip?"

The boys thought Dr. Lovejoy was charming and goofy and serious and smart all at the same time. They both instantly liked him.

"He is pretty funny," Wylde said. "Maybe I can even be talked into going to church on Sunday." Castilia looked at Wylde in amused surprise. "But then again, he wasn't THAT funny." They laughed and headed across the street to the Thrifty Mart.

They played a few video games until they blew all of their money. The games never lasted long enough. Castilia was wise enough to spend some of her money on candy and soda which she reluctantly shared with her brothers after their impetuous lack of forethought.

They emptied their collective pockets and wandered back toward the grocery store to find their mother who was just coming out of the door with a grocery cart full of food, headed toward the minivan.

"Oh good," Mom said, "I wasn't looking forward to wandering about looking for the three of you. Let's go." They all helped load the bounty into the hatchback of the minivan and got into the car for the short ride home.

"Samson, I almost forgot, I met the father of a friend of yours in the supermarket. His name was, umm...Minch...no.

Finch. He was a nice man. I told him you would be happy to have a playdate with his son any time. He was a very interesting man. He's some sort of professor."

"Good God NO, Mom." Samson protested. "Seriously, you can't be serious. This is a disaster. Argus Finch is my arch enemy. Please tell me you didn't invite them over."

Samson's Mom hesitated for a moment and said, "Ummm. Well, I kind of set something up for Monday. He said it was his day off and he didn't know what to do with his son. He seemed sort of helpless."

"He didn't know what to do with him because he is a gorilla! The boy has a mustache for goodness sake and he hates me! Why did you do this? You really can't make this happen. I will kill myself." Samson implored.

"Oh, Stop being so melodramatic." Mom retorted, "he can't be that bad."

"Are you kidding?", Samson interjected, "he hits third graders for fun to warm up for the sixth graders. The boy has no mercy or morals. It's like having a playdate with a hippo," Samson said. He was so riled up at this point he was starting to have an anxiety attack which made him sweat and shake. He needed to get out of the car and run around for a while.

Luckily, the short trip home was just that, short. Mom told everyone to help unload the car, but Castilia looked at her vexed brother and softly said, "Go. We'll take care of it." At that Samson bolted from the car toward the quiet forest beyond. Castilia and Wylde took the groceries into the house and appeased their mother. They then went outside to look for Samson equipped with a little snack.

They found Samson up on the knoll, high in the old oak tree. The wind was blowing his long blond hair around his head. He would always climb higher than anyone else could, or frankly, wanted to. The sky seemed to be the place he was the most at ease and where his short temper would defuse. He was safer there than anywhere else.

He climbed down a while later. Castilia and Wylde had made a picnic with the snacks and a blanket they brought and were chilling out at the base of the tree. Samson turned to each and apologized to his siblings. They offered him bites of fruit and bread which he hardily accepted. After he filled his belly, he felt more normal. Castilia could see the calm returning to his face and asked him if he was all right.

"Yeah, I think I've calmed down now. It's just, that guy really gets to me. Do you think he'd really come for a playdate?" Samson said with round, teary eyes.

"Doesn't seem likely, does it?" Castilia proposed. "He seems like a creep to me. but if, somehow the adults manage to actually let this happen, I've got your back."

They enjoyed the sunny afternoon lounging under the tree, not doing much of anything. Once the sun started to dip low in the sky, they gathered their things and made the trek back to the house. Thisbe was probably back from gymnastics and would be wondering where they all were.

When they arrived at the house they noticed they had a visitor who apparently drove the small white Ford Focus that was parked in the driveway. They all careened into the house like a herd of buffalo, stampeding into the mudroom, leaving a trail of backpacks, shoes, and trash in their wake.

"BACK, BACK!" their mother yelled as they sped into the house. "Clean it ALL up!" she shouted. They forced their momentum into reverse and headed back to the mudroom to put everything in its place. It took only a few seconds.

"Why they can't do anything on their own, I'll never know. They're like a pack of wild animals. I'm afraid they can't be let loose into society for some time." she said jokingly to her visitor.

Dr. Lovejoy laughed heartily and welcomed the children as they re-entered the kitchen after cleaning their mess. Thisbe sat with her mother, quietly sipping on lemonade enraptured by Dr. Lovejoy.

"Hey! I want some lemonade," Samson said loudly as he entered the room.

"Excuse me?" said his mother as she gave him the evil eye and nodded toward Dr. Lovejoy.

"Oh... sorry. Hello Dr. Lovejoy," Samson corrected himself and extended his hand in greeting. Dr Lovejoy took his hand and gave him a firm but vigorous hand shake.

"Hello, young man. Nice to see you again." Dr. Lovejoy said with his brilliant smile.

"Now may I have some lemonade?" Samson said to his mother, who ignored him as the others greeted the visitor. Only after proper manners had been attended to did mom start to pour the lemonade.

After everyone received a glass of lemonade and settled around the kitchen island, Mom said, "Dr. Lovejoy stopped by today to encourage us to join him this weekend at his church."

"Yes, I think you all will find it very interesting. I hope you will all come and start some interesting discussions. I would be pleased to hear your thoughts," he said as he winked at Castilia.

"Why do you care what we think? We are not exactly evangelical," Castilia said pleasantly.

"That is precisely why I care what you think," Dr. Lovejoy answered. "It is easy to preach to like minded individuals - there is hardly ever any disagreement or derision. Only a very precious few parishioners will question their pastor. There is very little dialog. Dissension allows for differing viewpoints to be heard and can often strengthen an argument."

"I didn't think Christianity was known for its open-mindedness," Castilia retorted sarcastically.

"Castilia! Watch your manners." her mother scolded and apologized to Dr. Lovejoy. "You'll have to forgive her, her father puts all kinds of ideas in her head."

"But that is exactly the frankness I crave," Dr Lovejoy emphasized the word 'crave' and drew it out as he turned his head to Castilia and held her gaze with a large smile. "And I must admit," he began again, "that Christianity has its tarnished past, but we must remember that every church is a collection of humans. And humans, as we all know, make mistakes, and some can be quite large." He took a drink of his lemonade and looked at all of the children.

"I like to encourage young people to think for themselves and follow their own paths. I believe that all paths lead to God in some form or another. The Bible says man is made in the image of God and therefore he takes a different image for each man...or woman, of course." He winked at Thisbe who blushed and said nothing. "My path has led to you at this moment and I am sure there is a reason for it. God works in mysterious ways, as the old cliche goes. Perhaps I am being tested, or perhaps you are." he said as he waved his hand in front of them all, hitting the lemonade pitcher as he finished his graceful swoop, almost toppling it off the counter. He clumsily tried to catch it but knocked it again with his hand which sent it flying toward the floor. Samson appeared from behind him faster than seemed possible to catch the pitcher just before it hit the ground as lemonade still went flying all over the floor. Lovejoy looked amazed as they all stood stunned as Samson held up the pitcher in victory drenched in lemonade. The silence was broken by a hearty laugh emanating past Lovejoy's shiny white teeth. They all broke into a wild roar of laughter.

"See." Dr. Lovejoy said at last, "Sometimes our mistakes are corrected with divine intervention!" he laughed again. "I thank you for your youthful reflexes, Samson, and if Daisy has a mop, I'd be happy to wash away my sinful behavior."

"Oh please, Dr. Lovejoy, don't think a second thought about it. Accidents happen. Anyway, I'll just make one of the kids clean it up so it's really no bother." Mom snickered as the kids laughter died away abruptly at the thought of the chore and immediately began to hide behind one another to avoid being chosen. Dr. Lovejoy reiterated his request that they all come join him this Sunday as Mom followed him to the door. When she returned to the kitchen, not a soul could be found. She picked up the nearly empty unbroken pitcher, smiled to herself, and headed to the pantry to get the mop.

That night at the dinner table the kids told their father about Dr. Lovejoy's visit and the things he said.

"That doesn't sound like any preacher I've ever met," Dad said with curiosity. "Perhaps we all should pay him a visit this Sunday." Dad's statement was met with a groan from the boys around the table.

"Are you kidding?," Samson said,"you're supposed to back us up on this. Didn't you say 'Church is for suckers?'"

"First of all, I'm pretty sure I didn't say that, and if I did you've probably taken it all out of context. Secondly, it does sound like something I would say, doesn't it? Anyway, my objection to most organized religion, as you know, is the rigidity of the dogma and reliance on faith. This Dr. Lovejoy seems, at the very least, capable of acknowledging another point of view. I also don't see anything wrong with going to church for one Sunday to check it out. Castilia and Thisbe both gave it the thumbs up when they went so that's good enough for me."

"Hey!," Mom shouted, "I told you last week he seemed interesting."

"Yeah, but you say that about every one of those things you visit, so your opinion doesn't hold much sway. Remember the People's Christian Love Festival you dragged me to."

"Oh my gosh, Sam, that was nearly 20 years ago," Mom said in exasperation. "you're never going to let me live that down."

"We almost got drugged and kidnapped and taken to some religious compound up in the Adirondacks." Dad laughed. "It's hard to forget that."

"What?!" all four kids piped in unison.

"Your mother took me to this weekend revival she read about in some hippie magazine and it turned out to be one of those really fundamentalist revivals where they talk in tongues and dance with poisonous snakes. It was quite fascinating I must admit. Kind of like watching those horrible reality TV shows that are infested with sad crazy people that you can't stop watching. That is until the leader, who I swear looked just like Jim Jones, with the greasy black hair and sunglasses, jumped up from the stage and hopped through the snakes to the front of the congregation who were all up dancing and clapping their hands and speaking in tongues. The preacher jumped around and pointed at your mother and said 'YOU' really loud. Everyone around her started clapping and grabbing her and pushing her up front telling her she was so lucky. This pretty much completely freaked me out and I grabbed her arm and started pulling her back at which time other people started surrounding us and pushing up both up to the front. I thought we were doomed and got really scared. The only reason we were able to get out of there was that one of the snakes bit the Jim Jones guy on the leg and he collapsed right there on top of the other snakes who all started biting him too. This caused pandemonium in the tent. Everyone swarmed the front to help the guy, at which time we got the hell out of there. It was one of the craziest experiences ever!" Dad finished with a snort and a laugh.

"Who's Jim Jones?" Wylde asked.

"Yeah, who is that?" the others said.

Mom and Dad looked at each other and rolled their eyes like they do when they give some obscure reference they think everyone should know and then said to google him like they always did. Castilia would, of course. Then she would tell the rest who he was. Most times, just like this one, it didn't seem to be anything really important, but Mom and Dad aways thought these nuggets of obscure information were valuable for some reason.

CHAPTER 14

The Flame

Saturday rolled around and the kids had various things to do in the morning, but all were back at the house for lunch and were left with a whole afternoon to kill as Mom and Dad were going out to have a massage and date night. That meant that Ms. Clark would be coming over to feed them dinner and make sure none of them escaped into the night to do something stupid.

They all headed out of the house to go fishing at the pond. It was a hot day, the dogs had already hunkered down under the porch, so nothing much would be biting, but fishing was better than cleaning up the chicken coop or weeding the garden or any other number of things they might get forced into doing if they were in too close a proximity of the house. They weren't in any hurry to get to the pond and wandered about aimlessly for a while. Chasing a toad here or a rabbit there. Wylde found a spotted salamander under a rock that was near a drainage ditch that was of pretty good size. That was a rare find and they all enjoyed holding the slimy creature before carefully returning him to his home. After a while they all found themselves traversing the knoll. They weren't paying much attention to where they were going. Samson and Wylde were discussing the possibility of recapturing the spotted salamander and how they might house him in their room. Castilia and Thisbe were arguing if Katy Perry or Lady Gaga was a better singer. So it was a great surprise when, "THUNK," Wylde's foot hit something that made a familiar sound. It was particularly surprising because they were no where near the location they found the door before. It was curiously obvious to everyone that it was in a totally different position.

"So I guess this thing just moves around, huh?" Samson stated the obvious.

"It's inexplicable," Castilia said, trying to be nonchalant.

"Couldn't wait to try out your new vocabulary word?" Samson said and crinkled his nose trying to look unimpressed.

"I nailed it!" Castilia giggled.

"Thunk, thunk," Wylde stomped his foot on the ground again. "Should we?" He looked around with a mischievous grin as the others nodded in excitement.

"Do we have the rope ladder?" Thisbe asked Wylde who was usually in charge of such things.

"Yeah, actually we do. We tied it up to the oak tree the last time we were over here, I'll go get it.

Wylde dashed off to retrieve the ladder as the others uncovered the portal. When he got back they had the circular door open and ready.

They secured the ladder to a tree nearby and threw it down into the hole. Wylde was given the honor of the first decent this time because he had his small pocket LED flashlight which was the only light source they had since they had not planned to visit the Chamber today. Fortunately the sun was high and bright and flooded the oculus making the small flashlight unnecessary. As they reached the bottom they each wandered inadvertently around gazing at the murals on the walls. Each eventually settled in front of their favorite: Samson to Fire, Castilia to Water, Thisbe to Wind and Wylde to Earth. The chamber was quiet as they studied the murals. Castilia brought her diary and sat on the sandy floor and began sketching the walls. Wylde took out his magnifying glass and was closely studying all of the painted animals on the wall. Thisbe was twirling about trying to emulate the painted patterns of the wind and air. Samson was standing perfectly still as if in a trace in front of the fire painting. The afternoon sun was making its way across the round room to the foot of the wall in front of Samson. The bright light brought out the delicate detail of the painting and make the fiery patterns seem to glow. Samson could feel the energy of the sun in his body, the warmth flowed though his veins. He felt fantastic. As the sunlight ascended the wall it seemed to pause on an image of a human figure floating in the midst of swirling flames. The figure had its elbows tight to its body with forearms extended perpendicular to its body. Small balls of fire hovered above its upward facing palms. Samson looked at his palms and then assumed the same position as the figure on the wall slowly turning his palms upward. His body became rigid. He could feel beads of sweat forming on his brow as all of his conscious was focused on the brightly lit figure before him. He was staring into the eyes of the figure and could feel the sunlight on the back of his neck. His gaze lifted slightly as his back tensed and...

"What are you doing?" Castilia said matter of factly from behind him. "You look really freaky."

"Huh?" Samson said coming out of his trance. "Oh, I was, um... I was..." He was disoriented and even a little dizzy, unaware of what put him in this state. He felt really weird and emotional.

"It looked like you were trying to imitate that figure there on the wall," she said raising her eyebrow and forming a half smile with her mouth. She did this just before she was going to make fun of someone.

"Listen, leave me alone. I was just looking at the painting." Samson said defensively, still feeling weird, like all his emotions were bubbling to the surface.

"You looked like you wanted to kiss the painting." Castilia continued judgmentally as her smile began to grow.

"I wasn't kissing anything.. I was just trying to figure out what the painting means."

"Do you think if you kiss it, the meaning will snap into your head?" Castilia chided her brother.

"I'm going to snap your head in a minute," Samson retorted.

"We all know you can't snap."

"I can too snap!" Samson said. He was getting aggravated. He knew his sister was just having fun at his expense, but he couldn't help walking right into her trap. He always did and she knew just what to do to push his buttons.

"You can't snap. You've never been able to do it." With that she gave him her best "oh no you diddint" face, crossed herself with her right hand, and threw it up in the air with a loud snap. Thisbe and Wylde were watching the exchange now and began to laugh.

"I can too snap, I just choose not to." Samson said growing red in the face, his temper rising, losing control of his emotions.

"Whatever... Talk to the hand." Castilia continued.

This always aggravated Samson to no end. His sister was the furthest thing from ghetto but she was really good at doing this routine. Typically when she did this to someone else, Samson was rolling on the ground laughing, but when it was his turn it made his blood boil because he knew she was just taunting him. There were few things that Samson couldn't do, and snapping his fingers well was one of them. He just couldn't make it work and his sister often had great fun with this fact at his expense.

"I can snap! And I will!!" Samson said now in a rage - he raised his hand high and flung it toward the floor as he pressed his middle finger hard across his thumb. The action, as always, did not make a sound, but something completely unexpected and miraculous happened.

"HOLY CRAP!" Wylde yelled and jumped back.

A ball of fire now engulfed Samson's right hand. It burned a bright yellow and orange and lapped lazily toward the ceiling as if it was completely natural for a flame to be surrounding someone's hand. It didn't hurt. It felt good in fact. Everyone stood aghast with eyes wide and mouths hanging open in shock. Everyone including Samson. He slowly moved his hand and watched the flames change shape as he moved. They were all mesmerized by the event and eventually got comfortable enough to move a little closer.

"Are you OK?" Is this hurting you?" Thisbe finally broke the silence.

"Um, yeah. It doesn't hurt at all. It actually feels good, like a warm bath." Samson said, still rotating his hand and staring at the flames.

Castilia was entranced with the glow radiating from his skin. A blend of colors ranging from blue and red to yellow and everything in between danced upon his hand. She recalled a familiar affect in their backyard fire pit on cool nights while roasting marshmallows. Castilia slowly walked to Samson and stretched out her hand toward the flame in his hand.

"Ow!" she yelled recoiling her hand quickly. "Well, it's really fire," she continued, shaking her hand and blowing on her fingers.

Samson took his left hand and pushed it into the flame to no ill effect. He then separated his hands leaving both of them ablaze.

"This is really cool." he said.

"Can you put it out?" Thisbe asked.

"I don't know. I'm not really sure how I even got this started." he said quizzically.

"Your necklace is on fire." Thisbe said meekly. She was getting upset again.

"It's not on fire," Castilia corrected. "It looks like its just glowing really hot. Its definitely burned your shirt again. Mom's going to be pissed."

"Crap, how do I stop this?" Samson said, now worried he was going to have to do his laundry for a week because he ruined another shirt.

"Try thinking you want it to stop," Castilia suggested.

"I've been thinking that since you told me my shirt was on fire." Samson said.

"Try thinking about water," Thisbe proposed.

"That just makes me need to use the bathroom," Samson said, frustrated.

"Why don't you just go over to the pool and stick your hands in the water?" Wylde said pointing at the pool of water in the center of the room.

"Yeah, OK." Samson said as he walked cautiously toward the pool. He gingerly knelt down and pushed his hands in the water. The flames were instantly dowsed and steam rose into his face. He pulled his hands out twisting them back and forth so he could inspect both sides of each hand. They were unharmed, unblemished, and perfectly normal.

"Awesome!" he said with amazement. He soundlessly snapped his fingers and once again his right hand was engulfed in flame. He doused it and steam rose toward the hole in the ceiling a second time.

"Awesome!" he said louder. He snapped his fingers and ignited his hand again. He paused and thought for a minute, scrutinizing his flaming hand, and then snapped his fingers a second time and the flame was extinguished.

"SUPER COOL!!!" he yelled. Everyone was very impressed.

"How'd you do that?" Wylde asked.

"The friction of my fingers seems to be the on/off switch."

Almost simultaneously, Castilia, Thisbe and Wylde all looked at their hands and gave a cautious snap. Three loud snaps rang in the air. But that was the extent of it. They all erupted in laughter.

"Dude, you're like the Human Torch," Wylde said excitedly. "My brother is the Human Torch!"

They spent the rest of the day down in the chamber watching Samson ignite and extinguish his hands. Until Castilia announced, "It's getting late, we better get back or Ms. Clark will have the police looking for us."

They all reluctantly climbed the rope ladder to the top and closed the door. Once up on the knoll Samson gave another silent snap but much to his chagrin, his new found gift seemed to leave him at the chamber threshold. They could hear Ms. Clark ringing the bell to return home and they scurried away in wonder at the day's discovery.

CHAPTER 15

The Sermon

The next morning was Sunday and as promised they were all rounded up and forced into presentable, unstained, and untorn clothes to go hear Dr. Lovejoy's sermon. The girls loved any chance to dress up, so they busied themselves getting ready without a word of complaint. The boys, however, were a much different story. Both Samson and Wylde were having trouble finding anything clean that was not torn but still fit. It wasn't until Wylde wandered into the kitchen with four inch high waters and a dirty shirt that mom was forced to intervene.

"I don't think I've ever even seen you wear this and it has a huge dirt stain on it. It's brand new. I can still see the creases from the packaging. How do you get something dirty that you've never worn?" Mom said frustrated as she hopelessly rummaged through Wylde's closet. Wylde looked bewildered as always and muttered under his breath 'I don't know' and 'I didn't do anything' as his mother continued her tirade.

"Have you been burning your clothes!" she exclaimed incredulously at Samson holding up two shirts with holes burned near the neck. "I can't believe you walk around like this. It's embarrassing."

She finally found clothes that she thought didn't, at least, as she put it, make them look like construction workers after a long, hot day of work.

Samson had to settle for some plaid pants he never wore because they were pink and green and blue and he hated them. They were also two sizes too small at this point and rose well above his ankles. Luckily he found a white knit shirt that had a small stain in the back that you couldn't see when he tucked it in his pants. His brother was not so lucky. He had absolutely no clean clothes anywhere so he ended up wearing blue pants with small red lobsters on them that he got as a gift last Christmas with a matching belt from one of his crazy aunts that somehow got the impression he liked lobsters. He also had to settle for THE pink shirt. The one that Samson received a year back but managed to avoid wearing completely because he hid it in the very end of the closet behind a large sweater which his mother only now found during her frantic search. It was now too small for Samson but still too big for Wylde. Because of the complete lack of options, Wylde was stuck with the pink shirt. Regardless of the absurdity of the outfits, they both quietly and obediently dressed themselves lest they really feel the wrath of their already perturbed mother. They looked ridiculous and this fact was repeatedly pointed out by their beautifully appointed sisters at every opportunity.

When Dad came down the stairs he immediately started laughing. "Daisy, you can't be serious. They look ridiculous." This support from their father gave the boys a glimmer of hope. They looked like sad puppies waiting for a bone.

"You are welcome to go up to their room and find another suitable solution if you like," she said shortly.

"Whoa, slow down there, let's not get crazy. They look fine. It's only an hour and at the very least, they can keep me entertained." He said as he started laughing again. At this the boys moaned as they knew their fate was sealed. "Everyone in the van!"

They got to the church and had a hard time finding a place to park. It was packed. They began wondering if there was some sort of special event today and asked some other churchgoers on their way in. They all said that it was just a typical Sunday, but since Dr. Lovejoy took over attendance was way up. There was electricity in the air, an excitement that they wouldn't have associated with a Sunday church service. They managed to find a seat for everyone in a pew toward the back. When the service started people were standing in the back as the organ filled the lofty room with music.

After a couple of hymns, the lighting of some candles and reading a few passages from the Bible, Dr. Lovejoy stood and walked to the lectern.

"Good Morning everyone" he began with a gracious smile. He paused and surveyed the room, nodding here and there in recognition. "God gives us everything!" he said throwing his hand and pointing his finger to the sky. He said this with such vehemence that many in the congregation snapped to attention. Dr. Lovejoy gave another large smile before continuing.

"Our strength, our resolve, our love. He gives us all of these things and we must learn to use them as he would want. Some of us are granted gifts in our lives from one time or another and it is what we do with these gifts that define us." Samson was barely paying attention at this point, but that sentence grabbed his attention. He looked up at Dr. Lovejoy at this point and would swear he winked at him.

"Did you see that?" Samson whispered to Castilia.

"What?" She said

"He winked at me."

"Don't be ridiculous. Hush." and she turned her attention back to the speaker.

"If we look to Isaiah Chapter 40 Verse 31, we see one of my favorite verses. 'But those who hope in the Lord will renew their strength. They will soar on wings like eagles; they will run and not grow weary, they will walk and not be faint.' Wow. That sounds pretty good. What else do we really need? Soar like eagles? Run and walk without growing weary? Who wouldn't want that? It sounds like a superhero. But I'm pretty sure Isaiah doesn't mean that God will make all of us superheroes - some of us sure," he said with a laugh. "There are special cases, but Isaiah is saying that we can all receive a gift. It is indeed a gift. But it is how we use these gifts that determines our value in life. And how are we to receive this gift? It's simple: Hope in the Lord. That's it. Hope in the Lord. But you might say to me, 'Dr. Lovejoy, I lost my job or I didn't get on the football team or I broke a nail just after I paid for a manicure.'" This was met with several giggles for which he paused and smiled. Dr. Lovejoy was clearly a showman and knew how to work the crowd. His charisma was in full affect. "How can I continue to hope in the Lord? Hope is how we appreciate life. Hope is the key to happiness. We hope every second of every day. I look upon the blue sky and hear the melodic sounds of birds singing gayly in the trees and smell the sweet fragrance of flowers in bloom. How can that not fill you with Hope? Hope that this day is better than the last, that the next will be better than this. Hope that we are able to live in the world and enjoy its wonders. Hope that I will be able to use God's gifts to their fullest potential. Hope that I am a good person. It is this hope in the Lord that allows us to use the gift of strength to be a good person. Philippians Chapter 4 Verse 13 says, 'I can do everything through him who gives me strength.' I can do EVERYTHING through him. Hope in the Lord is your guide through the wilderness of Life. Hope in goodness, in strength, and in Him.

I always find it helpful to look at things from different perspectives. It helps solidify your understanding and also creates empathy for another point of view. I was speaking to someone the other day who does not subscribe to our Christian notion of a God in heaven. We have had several discussions about the validity of a Specter in the sky as she calls Him. Yet, when we discussed the beautiful day, she mentioned how grateful she was to be a part of this wonderful thing called Nature. She described the relationship of all things to one another. She spoke of harmony and hope and how all thing are interconnected. She says she pulls her strength from this relationship. I say tomayto, you say tomahto." At this moment, Dr. Lovejoy subtly directed his gaze to the pew the Presleys occupied. As they would later discuss, they all felt as if he was speaking directly, individually, to them. "It is the same thing. The face of God is the Sun, or the Moon, or the swaying grass, or a gray-haired bearded old man. It makes no difference, it's all semantics. Hope is the key. When you lose your way, you lose Hope, you lose God, you lose the ability to soar on the wings of eagles. We have the power to define our own destinies through hope and our actions with the gifts we are given. We are given great power, we must be responsible with this power to keep Hope alive."

Dr. Lovejoy smiled at this conclusion and ended, "please turn your hymnals to page 236 as we sing, 'A Mighty Fortress is Our God.'"

At the conclusion of the service, all of the blue-haired old ladies sprinted down the aisle to be the first to say hello to Dr. Lovejoy. The Presleys slowly made their way out of the church. As before, Dr. Lovejoy was swarmed by the regular parishioners and the Presleys made their way down the steps and headed down the street to their car.

"Well, what did you think?" asked Dad to no one in particular.

"I thought he was talking directly to me," Samson said.

"What? Me too." Thisbe agreed.

Castilia and Wylde both nodded.

"I actually thought he was just staring at my clothes, I was a bit embarrassed." Wylde said as the others laughed heartily.

"That is the sign of a great orator," said Dad as they reached the car, "he does have a gift, for the lack of a better word. I thought it was an inspiring message that holds true for any belief system. Hope and Love make the world go round. Power, strength and responsibility all go hand in hand."

On the ride home, Castilia leaned over to Samson and whispered, "kind of makes our discovery a whole lot less awesome and a whole lot more scary." She had a worried look on her face and added. "We are going to need a lot of hope."

After they got home and changed, they all headed outside to enjoy the rest of the day. They spent much of their time up in the old oak tree contemplating the ideas of hope, power and responsibility.

"It can't be an accident that we found the Chamber and Samson now has this ability to handle fire. I think this is just the tip of the iceberg. Its a little scary to think about what we have been chosen for," Castilia posited.

"What makes you think we've been chosen for anything. Why can't it be that it's just a cool discovery." Samson argued.

"Are you kidding? Don't be an idiot. This is big, much bigger than us. We have to get ready for what's coming." she said.

"What's coming? What do you mean what's coming? There's nothing coming. Don't be ridiculous." Samson said, dismissing his sister as he normally did.

"I'm with Samson, I think you are way over reacting. It's only Samson anyway, none of us have been affected by the chamber so it has to be a coincidence." Wylde added.

"Listen, I know you boys don't like to think past the next meal you are getting but there is something going on here that we can't see. All these things are connected, there is no such thing as coincidence. Especially with something like this. This has happened for a reason. We just don't know what that reason is yet." Castilia was clearly very worried and was getting upset, which of course was getting Thisbe upset.

"Do you think it is dangerous?" Thisbe said tearing up.

"See, look what you are doing. You're getting Thisbe all upset for no reason. Let's just drop it for now, OK?" Samson turned to Thisbe, "Don't listen to her Thisbe. Everything is fine. The sun is shining and Mom is cooking a big lunch today."

"I see your mind is on the next meal, just like I said," Castilia said with a pleased grin on her face.

"What? I'm hungry." Samson replied with a laugh.

About that time they heard the dinner bell chiming in the distance.

"Last one home is a rotten egg!" Wylde shouted as he jumped off the lowest branch and tore off toward home.

"HEY! I'm the highest one up, wait up!" Samson said from high in the tree and began quickly descending.

"Too bad for you!" Thisbe and Castilia said over their shoulders as they followed Wylde down the trail.

"I'm still going to catch you!" Samson said as he leapt down from the tree. His bare feet hit the ground running as sparks seemed to emanate from his heels. He beat Thisbe and Castilia back home and almost caught up to Wylde.

"I think he's getting faster," Castilia said to Thisbe as he blew past them, leaving them in a cloud of dust.

"That's probably a good thing, isn't it?," Thisbe said as the wind suddenly picked up and blew the dust away.

"I hope so." Castilia said as she went in the house to eat. "I hope so."

CHAPTER 16

The Playdate

At breakfast the next morning, Mom reminded Samson that Argus was coming over for a playdate.

Samson's world crashed down around him. He had completely forgotten that his mother had make the huge mistake of inviting Argus Finch over for a visit. He woke up this morning thinking it was going to be a good day. He came downstairs hungry and began to devour his eggs and sausage. All of a sudden he lost his appetite. "Mommm, first of all, we don't call them playdates, it's a 'hangout.' And secondly, does he really have to come over? He's my arch nemesis."

"Samson, don't be dramatic. It's all set up. I talked to his Dad on Friday. Just try to be nice." Mom said.

"Will you call it off if I jab this fork in my eye?" Samson said holding up his breakfast fork. His mother just rolled her eyes and continued eating. "What I'm saying," Samson continued, "is that I would rather be blind in one eye than have a playdate, I mean, hangout with Argus Finch. You wouldn't want to subject me to a fate worse than losing an eye, would you?"

"Did you ever think that the boy lost his mother and has a father that works all the time and doesn't have many friends so he lashes out and causes trouble to get attention? Maybe you should think about someone else for a change and see if you can help them instead of exacerbating their misery." She said giving him her evil eye. "and yes, I know what happened two years ago."

"Castilia!" Samson yelled accusingly at her sister.

"What? You didn't say it was a secret," she said meekly.

"It doesn't matter," Mom said in her authoritative, this-is-the-end-of-the-discussion voice, "he'll be here after lunch and only for about an hour. Just take him outside and show him the chickens, play with the dogs or something and try to be nice for once."

"Fine." Samson's appetite was gone so he took his plate to the kitchen and skulked outside. He looked like a typical dejected twelve year old, moping around kicking rocks and the like for most of the morning. The minutes, unfortunately, flew by much too quickly. He had wanted the morning to last forever. Maybe if he was able to get to the chamber he could stop time or something, but he could not get everyone together and get them up to the knoll to try out his theory. Finally he got Castilia to agree to go up there, but by the time he rounded up Thisbe and Wylde, Castilia was no where to be seen. This went on for most of the morning.

"Oh my God! Its almost 11 o'clock!" Samson said in despair as he looked at his father's watch that he brought down to the kitchen.

"Samson, put that down. That's your father's favorite watch. Go put that back where it belongs?" Mom said.

"Mom, what time are they coming? This is torture! I'm not going to make it."

"Stop being so dramatic and go put back your father's watch."

"Really Mom, I'm feeling sick. AGGGH! it's 11 now!"

"Get outside! You are driving me crazy. Get!" Mom was advancing on his position so Samson retreated outside, but was no less anxious. He needed a distraction, but knew he would not be able to distract himself. Just at that moment, Wylde walked up with three large pumpkin-seed sunfish and a nice largemouth bass that he needed to clean.

"Hey, do you need any help with that?" Samson asked his brother with a look of desperation in his eyes.

"You've never asked to help me before, what's up?" Wylde asked inquisitively

"Argus is coming and I need a distraction to get my mind off of it. Please let me help." Samson pleaded.

"OK, go get some newspapers and a couple of knives." Wylde took his rod and tackle back to the shed.

Samson hurried into the house and grabbed the newspaper and two knives. He met his brother with the fish by the picnic table and laid the paper out for them to clean the fish. Wylde plopped the fish on the table and they each grabbed one. Samson was still very anxious, but the familiar task helped ease his mind a bit. He could remember showing his younger brother how to clean fish just last year. He glanced over to see how he was doing and saw something familiar.

"Wait a second, what's that?" Samson asked suddenly pointing his knife at his brother's fish.

"Its a sunny, stupid." Wylde insisted glibly.

"No, on the paper under the fish." Samson insisted and pushed the fish over. Under the blood stain and fish guts was a picture of some jewelry and artifacts with a heading that read "New Exhibit at the Maritime Aquarium."

"Oh, looks like some museum exhibit." Wylde said uninterested and continued pulling the guts out of the fish.

"Hold on, doesn't that look familiar?" Samson said pointing at the picture. He was pointing at a small medallion that looked very similar to the one he currently had around his neck. It seemed to be around the same size but the markings were different. Samson put his knife down and pushed Wylde's fish and the guts he just removed off of the picture to have a better look. "That looks like the water markings in the chamber. This is amazing." Samson said and quickly wiped his hands on his shirt and tore the picture and adjoining article out of the paper. "Castilia!" he called. "You'll want to see this! Castilia!"

He found Castilia up in her room reading a book about seals.

"EUUH! you smell like fish guts! Get out of here!" she screamed.

"Never-mind that, look at this!" Samson said, and thrust the torn article in front of her face.

"EEUUUUUH, that's disgusting! And it smells! You are gross. I'm telling Mom!" she said as she started to run out of the room.

"Hold on and look at the picture!" Samson yelled and grabbed her arm.

"EEUUUH! You've got guts on your hand! Don't touch me!" she shrieked.

"CASTILIA! Just look at the picture!," Samson's exasperation finally got her attention and she looked at the paper in his hand. Recognition hit her like a ton of bricks and she grabbed the paper from her brother and began reading the article.

"That's" she said with excitement.

"Uh huh." Samson knodded

"It's" she stammered again.

"I think so," Samson agreed.

"Unbelievable. We have got to check this out." She said with a huge grin. She had totally forgotten the paper she was holding inches from her face has fish blood and guts on it.

"SAMSON!" Mom shouted up the stairs. "Come on down, Argus is here."

In the excitement of the last few moments, Samson had completely forgotten about Argus again and his mothers call was like a punch in the stomach. He was crestfallen. He turned slowly and Castilia watched her brother leave her room.

"Dead man walking." he whispered and headed down the stairs.

Argus was big and ugly and standing in the foyer of his house. Unbelievable. Never in a million years did Samson ever think that a possibility. Argus's father was standing next to him talking to Mom. Argus, to his credit, looked none too pleased to be standing in the Presley home. As Samson descended the stairs, Argus looked up and gave Samson a half smirk as if to say, "yeah, I know. Unbelievable. How stupid are our parents." This was surprising to Samson as it seemed to be the first thing they had in common.

"Oh, here he is. Samson, of course you know Argus and this is Professor Finch." Mom said, but stopped and contorted her face. "Oh my God, what is that smell?" Mom looked at Samson and saw the streaks of blood and guts over his shirt and hands and a look of livid consternation washed over her face. "What have you?.." she began then stopped. "Did you?.." she started and stopped again. Looking him over one last time she said, "Get out of the house and take Argus with you." She finally finished and began apologizing to Professor Finch as Samson lead Argus outside without saying anything.

Once they were outside and out of earshot of the parents Argus slapped Samson on his back and said, "Dude, that was Awesome!" and started to howl in laughter.

"What?" Samson was floored. He did expect a slap of some kind but certainly not one of camaraderie. And did Argus just tell him he was awesome?

"I really didn't know what to expect coming over here but that was great. I've been trying to sabotage this whole thing all morning too but I never thought of dousing myself with fish guts. That is brilliant!" Argus was smiling and laughing. It was the first time Samson had seen anything other than a sneer on his big fat head. It was shocking. Samson didn't know quite what to say or do.

"I, um, well, um, I" Samson stammered and looked down at himself and started laughing too.

After the moment passed they looked at each other with blank stares.

"Look," Samson said. "We seem to be stuck with each other for an hour or two so we should make the most of it. Do you want to go climb the big oak tree over there?"

"Hell no." Argus stated flatly. The abruptness of it was startling to Samson but then Argus continued. "I don't climb trees. Look at me. Do I look like I climb trees? Do you want to hunt for snakes?"

"Really? I love to hunt for snakes!" Samson said relieved. "There is a great stone wall by the river that seems to be great place to look. Let's head over there."

On the walk over the boys chatted about snakes and other small animals. Samson was surprised to learn that Argus had a three foot python at home as well as a tarantula. Samson and Wylde, mostly Wylde, always had some sort of garter snake, frog or lizard they caught outside in a cage in their room, but nothing ever that exotic.

Argus was very knowledgeable about all kinds of snakes in the area, much more so than Samson. This lummox didn't seem to be such a dummy after all. They reached the stone wall and within five minutes Argus found a garter snake hidden in it. It looked to be about 30 inches long. Argus quickly grabbed the snake's tail and slid his hand down the snake to secure its head. He did this so quickly the snake barely had time to react. It was clear Argus was very adept at catching snakes. Typically, during a snake hunt outing Samson was lucky to see one or two snakes and even luckier if he was actually able to catch one. Samson was thought to be a tremendous snake hunter, but Argus not only found four snakes but caught and released each one. He was amazing. The afternoon swept by quickly and no sooner had they caught the fourth snake when the familiar tolling of the bell wafted through the air.

"That's my Mom, we'd better head back," Samson said.

The boys made their way back to the house and ran through the yard with the dogs running up to them, tails wagging in greeting. They entered the kitchen to find Mom and Professor Fitch chatting and drinking coffee. Samson grabbed his fathers watch that was still on the counter and found it was nearly three o'clock. They had passed the time amicably and actually had fun.

"Please don't mess with your father's watch Samson. How many times do I have to tell you?" Mom scolded, as Samson placed the watch back on the counter. "Did you boys have a good time?"

Samson caught Argus's eye and they had a moment of understanding. They both stammered some half-hearted answers like "it was OK" and "I guess" as they shuffled their feet and looked at the ground.

"Well, your hospitality has been much appreciated by us both." Professor Finch bowed to Mom. "We certainly would love to have you visit our home in the near future." At that surprise invitation Argus and Samson looked at each other with the familiar distain they were both used to. "Argus and I must be leaving now. Thank you so much for allowing us to visit. The conversation was stimulating."

As the Finches were leaving, Argus leaned over to Samson and whispered, "This changes nothing chump. I have a reputation to uphold." He then turned on his heel and walked out of the door.

The day's anxious events had exhausted Samson. After Argus left he headed upstairs to lay down, but his mother caught him halfway up the stairs and told him to get out of those smelly clothes and take a shower, which he gladly did, and then laid down to rest for a bit before dinner. His afternoon nap turned into a deep sleep. He had the same dream of flying over the farm, dashing and darting through the trees. He seemed to have more control this time. A slight movement of his hand would turn him this way and that. His feet seemed to give him altitude or make him dive. He was able to keep control while doing barrel rolls and loops. It was all very deliberate. Every movement of every joint made a difference in his flight, much like the lessons he learned in flight camp. It was the most liberating feeling of freedom he had ever known. "Soaring on the backs of eagles" was the best gift he could imagine.

CHAPTER 17

Maritime Museum

The next morning, Samson woke up to the sound of dogs barking. They were probably chasing a raccoon nosing around the chicken coop or some such thing. He could hear their excited barks get softer as they chased whatever it was away from the house. He sat up in bed, rubbed the sleep from his eyes, and realized he was famished. He couldn't wait to get downstairs and get something to eat. He bounded out of bed and rushed to the kitchen only to find it deserted. No one was awake. The sun was just barely up. It was five in the morning. Early to bed, early to rise and all that. Dad came down about five thirty as Samson was making quite the racquet trying fix something to eat and failing miserably.

"Here let me do that. You must be starved. You didn't eat dinner." Dad said as he took the pan away from Samson and started arranging everything to cook a proper breakfast. "Do you want pancakes?"

"Do I ever!" Samson said as his mouth started to water. Dad's famous pancakes were the best homemade pancakes this side of heaven. He usually only made pancakes on the weekends as he typically didn't have time during the week because he had to get to work. But given the early hour, he took out the flour and started creating his mix.

"So, how did the 'hang out' go yesterday? Mom said you made quite a spectacle of yourself. Did you really smear fish guts all over you?" Dad said with a grin, shaking his head and laughing to himself.

"Really, Dad, that wasn't what happened. Well, it is what happened but not the reason it happened. You see, Wylde caught these fish and I was helping him clean them when..." Samson began.

"Samson, it doesn't really matter, does it? I just want you to stop giving your mother such a hard time. Seriously, is it too hard to just do something nice for other people every now and then." Dad interrupted.

Because he didn't want to get into the reason for the excitement of the museum exhibit, Samson relented, "I guess not, I'll try harder next time."

"That's my boy." his Father said, proudly. "Now, do you want chocolate chips?"

Dad made a heaping pile of pancakes and Samson had his fill. Dad came down after getting ready for work and asked if Samson had seen his watch. Samson explained that it was on the counter yesterday but he didn't know where it was this morning. Dad asked him to look for it since he had to get to work. The others didn't venture downstairs until much later, but enjoyed the pancakes nonetheless. Samson made the most of the quiet morning and did some research regarding the new exhibit at the Maritime Aquarium. It had started the weekend before and was open for the next two weeks. When everyone had finished breakfast, they conspired to convince their mother to take them to the Aquarium that very day. Castilia was particular adamant that they get there as soon as possible. After they finished their chores they all cornered Mom to request the trip and argue their case, and surprisingly met absolutely no resistance.

"You know, I read about a new exhibit they have there and I've been wanting to go. That sounds like a great idea. Let's get ready and get on the road. Perhaps we will take a picnic for the beach afterward." she said warmly.

They all merrily readied themselves for an outing and were actually screaming for Mom to hurry up, instead of the usual other way around.

The museum was in an old brick warehouse that had been renovated a few years prior. An IMAX was added, and an indoor/outdoor seal exhibit as well. For a small-town Aquarium it was quite complete, and had sharks and rays, seals, turtles, otters and a number of local fish. The new exhibit was entitled "Lost Atlantis, Treasures of the Sea" and featured artifacts from various shipwrecks and dive sites from around the world. It was set up in the large main gallery of the Aquarium. This was a triple height space with the main stairs between the tanks that housed the boat that make the first solo excursion of the atlantic ocean as well as a couple of other small sea vessels of importance that they hung from the rafters like space ships. The Atlantis exhibit had several kiosks with models of the fabled city. There were images of mermaids and mermen that surrounded much of the space. Interactive exhibits asked questions about how humans could live underwater, and if we could grow gills. In the center of all this lay the glass enclosures that housed the lost artifacts.

Castilia walked directly to the case that housed the medallion they saw in the paper. Mom slowly perused the exhibit and was way behind her children.

"There it is." Castilia stated the obvious, glassy-eyed. It was a medallion the exact size of the one Samson wore around his neck, and was the same color. The markings were different, however, but looked extremely familiar. All of the items including the amulet had numbers that corresponded to an informational display above the case. While most items had a very descriptive paragraph of what it was and where it was found, such as, 'jewel encrusted hair pin worn by the Duchess of Cranbuckle and lost at sea when her ship the Pink Lily sunk in 1785 off the coast of Antigua. Recovered by David Mortenson aboard the Ocean Seeker in 1986' the amulet simply said,'metal medallion found off the Ivory Coast around 1972. Origin unknown.'

"It looks just like the drawings in the Chamber. There are the four wavy lines that look like a stream and then the curled lines that look like a breaking wave. and the tiny fish jumping and everything," Thisbe observed.

They were all leaning over the glass to get a good look when they noticed it began to glow. They gasped, and looked around relieved to find no one else around.

"Look at Samson's neck." Thisbe said quietly. A faint glow could be seen emanating from inside his collar. He stood up away from the enclosure and the glowing subsided. They noticed that the medallion inside faded as well. Samson leaned toward the enclosure again and the glow increased. As he pulled back the glow subsided once again.

"This is NOT a coincidence Samson." Castilia said defiantly. "These amulets are connected. This one is here for a reason. I can feel it."

"It's all very weird," Wylde said with trepidation, looking around to make sure no one was watching again.

"Are you thinking we need to get that amulet somehow?" Samson asked Castilia raising his eyebrows.

"I don't know," she said thoughtfully clearly weighing her options. "What I do know is that this is too coincidental to be coincidental."

"You're talking in circles and not making sense." Samson mocked.

"There's really no way to get a closer look at this anyway so we may as well drop it." Castilia said as their mother caught up to them.

"What did you find?" Mom asked.

"Just some interesting jewelry." Thisbe said with a smile and they all moved on.

The amulet, however, shimmered as they left, almost like a wink.

They all enjoyed the rest of the day at the beach and often mentioned the amulet in the Maritime museum. They came up with various hair-brained schemes on how to retrieve it. Wylde suggested learning a disappearing magic trick from that book on magic Samson checked out of the library a couple of weeks ago. He didn't quite understand that those tricks were slight of hand - they didn't actually make things disappear and reappear. They couldn't buy it or steal it. They couldn't even come up with a viable scenario where they would even be able to touch it. All of their speculation and scheming would prove to be pointless in the end anyway. The next few days bore out two remarkable events that none of them were ever able to explain.

* * *

They ended the day at the beach as the sun was setting. They were all tired and hungry. Mom needed to get everyone home to meet Dad and have dinner. When they arrived home, they found their Father in a frantic state and the house was a bit of a wreck.

"Good Heavens Sam! What on earth is going on here?" Mom exclaimed as she surveyed the mess.

"I can't find it Daisy. I've looked everywhere. That's my grandfather's watch." He said angrily as they walked in.

Mom slowly turned and looked at Samson. "What did you do with it?"

"What did I do with what?" Samson asked. He felt a strange tingle run up his back as if he were about to get blindsided.

"You know perfectly well what I'm talking about. You were playing with Dad's watch all day the other day and that's the last time I saw it," Mom said.

"What? Me? I didn't do anything with it." Samson honestly answered, but knew that it wasn't going to end well. His mom's ire was up.

"Did you put it back up on Dad's dresser like I told you to do?"

"Ummm... I think I ... Ummm..."

"It's a yes or no question," Mom said now crossing her arms, tilting her head, and raising her left eyebrow as she was wont to do just before an inquisition began.

"No, but I don't know where it is," he quickly began. "It was on the counter last time I saw it and I didn't do anything with it."

"OK, then where is it?" Mom was getting tense she and raising her voice. Thisbe, Blu and Wylde were watching with wide eyes. Wylde looked over at Castilia and with a worried look on his face slowly snuck out of the room. Castilia and Thisbe followed in short order. They all knew when the fireworks started anyone was liable to get burned if they were too close.

"How am I supposed to know?" Samson said raising his voice. "Last time I saw it was right here." He pointed in the general area of the counter.

"So it just walked away then?" Mom began sarcastically, "All by itself."

"I don't know!" Samson yelled.

"Are you yelling at me? Because it sounds like you are yelling at me." Mom said baiting her oldest son.

"No, I'm not yelling," he said cautiously." But I don't know where Dad's watch is."

"Then you better start looking. You're on restriction until you find it. No TV, no internet, no electronics!" Mom laid down the law.

"Mom." Samson pleaded. "I didn't have it. It's not me!"

"It is now. If I were you, I'd stop complaining and start looking." The discussion was over. Mom walked away, leaving Samson with his mouth open in disbelief and disgust at the injustice of it all. Dad gave Samson that "I'm so disappointed in you look" and turned and left the room without ever saying anything. That, of course, was even worse than a good tongue lashing. The parental guilt was overwhelming. Samson finally shut his mouth and began retracing his steps to try and figure out when the last time he saw Dad's watch. When he decided this was quite fruitless he began a random search of everything. It was pointless. He knew two things. He didn't have the watch and he didn't have a clue where it was.

CHAPTER 18

The Key

The next morning Samson was still treated to the agonizing silent treatment from his parents. They would not even look at him. Mom had left a long list of chores for Samson to begin his penitence. It was a very long list but he knew better than to complain as that would only make the list longer. Conversation that morning, however, took his mind off his troubles, if only for a moment.

"Didn't you go to the Maritime museum yesterday Daisy?" Dad asked while eating his oatmeal and reading the morning paper.

"Yes, there is a fascinating new exhibit there on shipwreck treasure. There are some really nice artifacts that have been discovered recently using digital and sonar technology. They had this whole display on how technology developed by James Cameron, you know the director, now helps with deep sea treasure hunting. The kids seemed to be particularly interested. We had a great time there."

"I thought you went yesterday. Apparently there was a burglary last night where someone tried to steal some of the items in the exhibit. A glass case was smashed and all the contents were stolen. The perpetrators went in and out in seconds and they don't have any leads."

The table was silent. Everyone was paying close attention now.

"Do you know what they took? Maybe we saw it." Mom continued.

"It says here that only a few small artifacts were taken out of a single display." Dad began. Castilia turned to Samson with a worried look on her face. Could the amulet be lost so soon after they discovered it? "The value of the items was unknown and the police seem perplexed that they took what they took and that's all that they took as there was apparently several items of great value right next to what they took." Dad continued.

Castilia and Samson looked at one another in shock. Their glances said they needed to talk. They nodded to Thisbe and Wylde, who also understood. As they, well, mostly Samson, cleared the table, they quietly and briefly discussed this new development.

"So do you think they stole the amulet?" Thisbe asked no one in particular.

"It's got be the amulet. That display had all of the miscellaneous items and most of them were small fragments of metal objects. None of that stuff was gold or jewelry or anything of value," Castilia said, clearly aggravated by the whole thing.

"Maybe Mrs. Goodwyn would know something about it," Thisbe said thoughtfully.

"That's a good idea, Thiz, but there is no way I'm getting out of the house any time soon," Samson said in dismay.

"I've got a playdate with Henry today so I'm out," Wylde answered.

"Well, I guess it's up to us, Thiz," Castilia said, and they began to formulate a plan.

Samson spent the day cleaning out the chicken coop, again. Washing this and that, splitting wood, and weeding the garden. There never seemed to be a lack of things to do around the house. The kids theorized that their parents deliberately planned out discipline to keep the property properly kept. Samson, because he was the oldest and most capable, tended to receive more of the backbreaking sentences and more often. The loss of the watch was perplexing. He spent much of his time now trying to retrace his steps from the last time he saw it and couldn't come up with anything other than he left it on the kitchen counter. No one else had been in the house other than his brother and sisters since that time, except Argus. He kept coming back to Argus. Today, anyway, he had plenty of time to think it through and also think about what to do about it.

In the meantime, Castilia and Thisbe rang Mrs. Goodwyn to ask if they might come by for a visit today. Mrs. Goodwyn sounded excited at the prospect of having visitors and asked that they come by for a mid-morning snack; perhaps around 10:30. The girls told their mother they were going to town to get some candy and whatnot at the Thrifty Mart and then they would visit their new friend. Mom thought it was a very generous idea and happily gave them permission. They pulled their bikes out of the barn and headed to visit Mrs. Goodwyn.

It was another hot summer day. They decided to save the candy run until after their visit to avoid melted chocolate in their pockets, and because they were running a bit late as Castilia couldn't find the right shoes. The ride through town proved to be sweaty and dusty, but they easily made it to Ferrall Road and parked their bikes by the front steps. Castilia took off her helmet and looked at her grimey face in her bike mirror. She didn't look too bad but began to rework her ponytail. As she was doing this she looked over at Thisbe who, once again, looked as if she had been idly walking through the park without a hair out of place and no sweat or dirt upon her person.

"Ugh. How do you do that?" Castilia asked disgusted.

"Do what?", Thisbe answered innocently.

"Look like you just stepped out of the shower and just blew out your hair even though we've both just climbed that awful hill on our bikes in this hot humid weather." Castilia said as they headed toward the front door.

"I have no idea what you're talking about," Thisbe answered with a smile and rang the bell.

Mrs. Goodwyn cheerily answered the door and had made herself properly presentable for the visit. She looked a bit like June Cleaver in an old pink sun dress with a matching belt and a string of pearls around her neck. Her eyes were still slightly foggy but twinkled with life. Her face was wrinkled and showed her age but looked healthy with rosy cheeks. She had fixed her silver hair very neat in a tight bun on the back of her head and wore matching pearl earrings that dangled from her loose lobes like wrecking balls. The house looked completely different than their last visit. It was bright and airy with the distinct smell of recent disinfectant still in the air.

"Hello girls," her husky voice sang a bit clearer this morning, "I'm so glad you've come, please come in, come in." She waved the girls past the threshold of the door and followed them to the living room where they saw she had arranged a proper tea for their visit.

"Your last visit was a much needed jolt of youthful vitality. I had forgotten that life is more than just soap operas and cold ham sandwiches. I did not realize how depressed and isolated I had gotten over the last few years. My daughter has been trying to get me up and out of the house for ages. I apologize for the way you saw me last." Indeed Mrs. Goodwyn seemed like a completely different person now: she had color in her face and even a bit of makeup. She seemed much taller and moved with a dignified, graceful air.

"You seem very healthy and your dress is very pretty." Thisbe complimented their host. "I love pink, but red is my favorite color."

"Why thank you, Thisbe. I haven't felt this good in years. Please sit down. Do you both like tea?" Mrs. Goodwyn asked.

"Do you have any honey for the tea?" Castilia asked. She loved honey, and sugar. Basically anything sweet was her favorite, but she particularly loved honey in her tea.

"Of course dear, let me go get it from the pantry." She retrieved the honey and poured them each some tea from the pot steeping on the table. Castilia loaded hers with honey and also added a lump of sugar because Mom was not there to stop her. Thisbe had some sugar and took a fresh cookie from the tray as well.

"These are delicious," Thisbe said taking another cookie from the tray, "did you bake these?"

"I had a feeling you would be calling upon me this week so I whipped up a couple of batches of cookies just yesterday as I was cleaning the house. It's taken me a while to get things back in order. It was an embarrassing mess. But I've slowly worked my way through the house the last week and it seems much more like home now. My daughter has been very pleased with my recent resurgence as well."

"How did you know we would be calling?" Thisbe asked. "We only decided to come this morning."

"Well dear, while I can't see or hear very well anymore, my intuition seems to be strong and more accurate than ever." She smiled and took a sip of tea.

"We have much to talk to you about. We visited the Chamber of Transition again and Samson was able to play with fire. It was really freaky but it didn't seem to hurt him. Fire surrounded his hand and he was able to flick it on and off. After one point, he actually seemed to be able to control it. He also has this medallion that glows when we are down there. Maybe that's why he seems to be the only one that has any reaction when we visit." Castilia explained.

Mrs. Goodwyn sat in silence for a moment and pondered this new information. She continued to look pleasantly at Castilia, but it was clear she was not looking at her. Castilia started to get uncomfortable at the eerie stare until Mrs. Goodwyn finally broke her trance and spoke again. "I think it is good that you visited the Chamber again, I also think you should go more often. Samson will need time to hone his skills. I'm not aware of the medallion, or its importance."

"We found another one at the Maritime Museum. This one is slightly different but I felt like I had a connection with it." Castilia said.

Again Mrs. Goodwyn sat in silence for an awkwardly long time staring into Castilia's eyes unblinking. Castilia was getting uncomfortable.

"You know, that's sort of creepy." Castilia said almost in a whisper. This seemed to snap Mrs. Goodwyn back to reality. She softly giggled.

"I'm sorry dear. I didn't mean to make you uncomfortable. I was just thinking." she giggled again and continued. "As I get older, I find my social graces deteriorating. It also takes my mind a moment to digest things. I still do not perceive the importance of the medallions. Maybe they are an amplifier or key of some sort."

"Key?" Thisbe asked. "Key to what?"

"Sometimes one needs help to find their path; a locked door blocks the way. Just as you helped me find the path I lost. I could not find the key to the door, you were my key."

They all sat for a while thinking about this. The fragrance of the chamomile tea surrounded and soothed them as they sipped in the comfort of the company. Then Mrs. Goodwyn's cloudy eyes turned sombre and her face more serious.

"I'm afraid things are not going to be as carefree and happy for you as they have been. I see dark storms approaching, particularly for your brother Samson," said Mrs. Goodwyn prophetically.

"Yeah, he got in trouble for losing Dad's watch. He's at home doing a ton of chores," Thisbe explained, not understanding the gravity of Mrs. Goodwyn's words.

"I don't think that's what Mrs. Goodwyn is referring to, Thiz. Is it Mrs. Goodwyn?" Castilia looked at her with worried eyes.

"I love Thisbe's trusting and optimistic nature. It is good that she has you as a sister, and you her." Mrs. Goodwyn answered. Thisbe looked at them both with a confused half smile, still trying to put together what she was talking about. Mrs. Goodwyn continued to look serious. "I see dark figures in and around Fox Hollow. They seem to want something; to bend and twist its purpose. Be wary of strangers and strange happenings."

Mrs. Goodwyn's words were not comforting at all and Thisbe was clearly shaken - tears began to well up in her eyes. "There, there dear. Now is not a time for tears, but for resolve and determination. You are fully capable of handling whatever is lurking in the darkness." At this Thisbe completely lost her composure and began sobbing into her hands. Mrs. Goodwyn placed a comforting hand on Thisbe's knee and looked to Castilia. She continued, "Castilia you will have to help your brothers and sister, particularly your sister. You know she can be very emotional, but that may very well be her biggest asset. You, however, are strong and rational. You will need your wits about you, I fear."

Castilia looked at Mrs. Goodwyn with a face full of disbelief. She jumped out of the chair wringing her hands and pacing the room. "You have got to be kidding. I'm twelve years old! This is crazy! What have we gotten ourselves into?"

"That, my dear, is a good question. It may, in fact, be THE question. Unfortunately, I do not have the answer at present. I do know this, you must learn and develop and grow. There is still time." Mrs. Goodwyn spoke in a calm melodic voice that helped calm Castilia. The lump in her throat began to shrink and her breathing calmed. She thought for a moment.

Castilia turned to Mrs. Goodwyn and asked, "We still have time for what?"

Thisbe had quieted her crying for the moment and looked to Mrs. Goodwyn with teary eyes. "I think for now, time is all you need. All things are discovered in time. More tea?"

Castilia was shaken out of her thoughtful gaze. "What?"

"Would you like more tea, dear? I find a nice cup of tea helps me think." Mrs. Goodwyn answered sweetly, like nothing she had just said was out of the ordinary.

Castilia shook her head trying to reconcile 'tea' and 'dark figures' in her head. It really wasn't working. She needed some fresh air and needed to get out of this stuffy old-lady house. She was flummoxed and forgot her usually good manners.

"No, I don't want more tea," Castilia said a little too brusquely. "I need some air. Thisbe let's go." She abruptly got up, stormed through the room, and headed out of the door. The door shut with a little more force than was necessary.

This startled Thisbe, who was embarrassed by her sister's ill manners even though she herself had just minutes before sat bawling into her hands. At this point, Thisbe had her senses about her and her head was clear. Crying for her was like rain - it washed away all of the dirt and haze and when it stopped all was clear and fresh. She felt much better.

"I'm sorry for Castilia, Mrs. Goodwyn. It was great seeing you today even if it was scary. Thank you for the tea. I hope you won't mind if we visit again." Thisbe said standing up.

"Of course, dear. I afraid many of our visits will end up just like this. You should run after your sister. Just like you need her, she too needs you." Mrs. Goodwyn said as she slowly rose to show Thisbe to the door.

"Let me help you clear this stuff before I go," insisted Thisbe.

"No, no. It frankly gives me something to do. You run along now. I expect I'll see you soon," she said as she opened the door and ushered Thisbe outside.

"Goodbye, Mrs. Goodwyn."

"Goodbye, dear."

Thisbe saw that Castilia's bike was gone. She couldn't quite believe her sister just left her. She never did that. Nevertheless, Thisbe got on her bike and headed down the driveway in search of her sister.

CHAPTER 19

The Hospital

Thisbe turned her bike down Ferrall Road after leaving Mrs. Goodwyn's house and began picking up speed down the hill toward town. After a few moments of the wind blowing in her face she noticed people running back and forth across the street at the bottom of the big hill. Someone was talking on a cell phone in the middle of the street making wild gestures with their free hand. Another person was kneeling next to something in the tall grass on the right side of the road. There was definitely an odd air of immediacy in their movements. Something was amiss. That was when she saw Castilia's bike in a crumpled heap about 5 yards away from the group. She hurried down the hill to find several adults running around, the one on the phone was shouting now. "a little girl, Yes!... Ferrall Street...Yes!...Please hurry!"

Thisbe screeched to a halt, jumped off her bike, threw off her helmet and ran over. She began to panic.

"That's my sister!" she screamed as she knelt down to find Castilia unconscious, with blood pouring profusely from under her helmet. Her leg was twisted in an impossible angle. She lunged to hold her but the adults grabbed her and held her back.

"No!," Thisbe screamed as she began to cry, "She's my sister." Thisbe's head began to spin. She stopped struggling as the woman who was holding her held her tight and said in a calm motherly voice, "Don't touch her, you could hurt her worse than she is, we've called 911." Thisbe gave in at this point and started crying. Through her sobs she imperceptibly asked "What happened?" as she heard the sounds of sirens coming in the distance.

The next few hours were really tough on Thisbe as the paramedics arrived and swarmed over Castilia, inserting needles and braces and tubes into her. Several policemen and firemen asked her questions she didn't really hear and couldn't remember if she had answered. She heard some of the adults saying things like "it was a dark blue sedan..." and "when I shouted at him, he calmly stood up and left."

The paramedics secured Castilia on a plank with orange straps and slowly carried her out of the ditch and into the awaiting ambulance. Thisbe was invited to ride with Castilia in the ambulance and they buckled her into a seat at the rear of the truck at Castilia's feet. It was incredibly frightening. The siren was going full blast as the paramedics continued to check and recheck Castilia. She looked horrible, with blood all over her face and an oxygen mask over her nose and mouth. Her neck was in a brace. The paramedics continued to poke and prod Castilia and shout orders to one another. The driver was on the radio reporting to the hospital that there was an incoming patient.

The ride was bumpy and Thisbe was getting jostled as they sped through traffic. Castilia was strapped down on the gurney so she couldn't move. Her left leg was in some sort of splint, while her right foot poked out from under the blanket they had placed on her. Thisbe reached out and held onto her sister's bare and dirty right foot. It was all she could do. When Thisbe touched Castilia's foot she felt a sharp chill run through her arm into her spine. She calmed herself after the initial shock and warmed her body through to her hand, chasing away the chill. All of a sudden, the ambulance got quiet and the paramedics finally relaxed and stared at the monitors. Castilia's heartrate slowed and became steady, her blood pressure leveled off and she seemed to be sleeping soundly. The paramedics looked at each other, grinned, then turned to Thisbe and said, "your sister's going to be all right." Thisbe squeezed her sisters foot in relief.

The next few hours were incredibly hectic, They made it to the hospital and wheeled Castilia quickly into the emergency room as another swarm of doctors enveloped her. Someone put a hand on Thisbe's shoulder and told her she couldn't come any further and left her standing at the threshold of two large gray double doors. Thisbe had no idea where to go or what to do next. She was worried and scared. She looked around with big worried eyes at the large room filled with strangers that all looked to be in various stages of misery.

"Hello," came a voice from behind her that startled her a bit, "I'm Officer Dunham. You must be Thisbe. Do you mind if I sit with you until your parents arrive and ask you some questions?"

Her parents. It hadn't yet occurred to her to call her parents.

"Oh my gosh, Mom and Dad. I need to call them." she said urgently to the police woman.

"Your parents have been notified and should be here shortly. Why don't you come over to my station and we can wait for them to arrive. Would you like some water?" she asked as she led Thisbe to a couple of chairs behind a nearby counter. Thisbe realize she was extremely thirsty and nodded yes to Officer Dunham.

Officer Dunham asked Thisbe a couple of questions and quickly learned that she didn't see anything other than the aftermath of the accident. Thisbe had some questions of her own.

"What happened to her?" she asked.

"Well, as far as I know it was a hit and run. Someone hit your sister and even got out of the car to check on her, then sped off. Two of the neighbors saw the whole thing. I'm sure we'll find the persons responsible in no time." Officer Dunham explained.

Thisbe nodded in disbelief. She really needed her Mom and Dad. Officer Dunham tried to comfort her with small talk while they waited but Thisbe didn't hear a word she said.

After what seemed like hours of staring at the floor and listening to the buzz in her head that was the soft voice of Officer Dunham, Thisbe was jolted to attention by the sound of her mother bursting through the room.

"Where's my baby!" Mom yelled. There was definitely panic in her voice which startled Thisbe. "Where's Castilia?!" Mom ran into the emergency room followed by Dad and the boys. They headed straight to the desk and a commotion ensued while Dad tried to calm Mom and get the necessary information. Samson and Wylde stood wide-eyed and slack-jawed as their clearly distraught mother was yelling at the nurses and doctors and anyone who would listen to get her to her daughter. Samson scanned the rest of the room until his eyes rested on Thisbe. He nudged Wylde and they both came running over to her. At the sight of her brothers running towards her she started tearing up again. Samson gave her a big hug and Wylde piled on as well. Suddenly, she was whisked up into the warm strong arms of her father who had finally gotten the doctors to lead mom to Castilia's bed. He lifted Thisbe in his arms and whispered in her ear, "You did good." Even though she thought she was out of tears, Thisbe started crying in earnest again. Her father held her until she calmed once again. He set her down on her feet, looked her in the face, smiled, and gave her a tender kiss on the forehead before rushing off to find Castilia and Mom.

"Take care of her, I'll be back in a minute." He said to Samson as he left the room.

CHAPTER 20

The Recovery

Castilia had indeed been hit by a car while she was riding her bike down the hill toward town. Admittedly she wasn't paying too much attention as she was deep in thought about her conversation with Mrs. Goodwyn. She said she was riding her bike and the next thing she remembers she woke up in the hospital with Mom hovering over her head.

She had a broken her left leg and had a soft cast up to her knee. She also had a concussion. Had she not been wearing her helmet, the crash might have killed her. She had an awful headache. She stayed overnight at the hospital so they could watch her. The doctors were worried about her concussion, but she made it through the night just fine. The next few days were very cloudy for Castilia, as the pain medication wore off and she began feeling her injuries.

She slept a lot and had strange dreams of black figures poking at her and tugging on her leg. The figures were hazy and left streaks of black in the air as they moved. They did not speak, but would buzz and bark to one another. They would rush up to her quickly and grab her neck and hands, feeling her like they were searching for something. It always ended the same way - the figures were chased away by a large white dog barking mightily, bearing his teeth. Castilia always felt like something was taken from her once the dark figures ran away, but the dog came and put his muzzle under her neck to help her up. She stood and immediately jumped into the stream that was now running right beside her. She felt the coolness of the water on her body and it felt clean and strong. She dove deeper and deeper into the water, leaving sunlight behind, her lungs beginning to strain. Keep the faith, it will be alright, she kept telling herself, but her lungs began to beg for air and she stopped and looked upwards to the distant light. The light was so far away, she would never make it, but she swam toward it, faster and faster. Her lungs ached, her throat constricted and started to convulse, but she remained calm. The light was growing brighter. She was almost there, she had to breathe. But then the light was gone. Panic slowly started to surface. She had to breathe, she had no choice. Panic surrounded her. She opened her mouth, water rushed in filling her lungs and she woke up.

"Weird." Thisbe said. "What do you think it means?"

"No idea." Castilia coughed. Her head still hurt, but mostly her butt hurt because she had to lay down on her back in her bed with her leg raised most of the time. The throbbing in her leg was getting less severe.

"So let me get this straight. Mrs. Goodwyn said there are 'dark figures'" Samson held up his fingers making quotation marks when he said 'dark figures,' casing the joint, and we need to be wary of strangers and strange happenings. Is that right?"

"Yes, that's exactly what she said," Castilia agreed.

"That's just great. Really helpful." Samson said sarcastically.

"Well, she did say that we need to visit the Chamber more often to practice," Thisbe said. She really liked Mrs. Goodwyn and didn't like it when Samson was being indignant toward her.

"Lot of good that does us now." Samson said, " Castilia's bedridden. How are we going to get in there?"

"Right. I didn't think of that." Thisbe said

"I'll be better in no time. I can't wait to go swimming again." Castilia said with a smile.

"Swimming? Are you crazy? The doctor said you'd be in a cast for 3 months. He said your leg was shattered." Samson scolded his sister. While he was grateful she was not hurt worse than she was, her broken leg was getting on his nerves already.

"That's nonsense. I'm too awesome to have a broken leg for that long." Castilia said with a smirk. "Plus, I really need a bath. I feel disgusting."

"You smell disgusting," Wylde chided with a giggle.

"Well, I guess I'll go look for Dad's watch while I'm waiting for you to walk again," Samson said as he slunk out of the room. Samson was still on restriction until he could find his Dad's watch, which had proven to be an impossible task. Samson hated looking for things. He hated losing things and he hated looking for them after he lost them. Mostly he hated losing thing because he hated looking for them. He really wasn't any good at looking for things. Something could be right in front of his face and he could miss it. Mom said it was in his genes. Samson thought that was because his Dad couldn't ever find anything either. Regardless, Samson performed this searching ritual every morning to no avail. Looking in drawers, pants pockets, under beds, under rugs, in the pantry, everywhere. It was truly getting ridiculous. He was never going to find that damn watch.

The next day Mom took Castilia back to the doctor to get a more permanent cast. The doctor seemed to be amazed at her rapid recovery and happily put on a waterproof cast at Castilia's request. The new fiberglass cast made it easier for her to get around even though she was not yet able to put any weight on her leg. Her leg still throbbed but she was able to get around the house for short periods of time. She would get tired quickly and still spent most of her time in her room, reading, with her leg up. Her siblings were helpful and Samson began to get hopeful that they may soon be able to revisit the Chamber of Transition.

Samson's punishment seemed never-ending and fruitless. He was never going to find the watch. It had disappeared. He had taken to following the dog around and poking sticks in his poo, just in case he ate it. "Desparate times call for desparate measures," he told Wylde after being caught in the act.

One morning after breakfast Samson began his search once again and hit all his usual spots. He started in the kitchen, then moved to his Dad's office, then to his closet. He had taken to searching all of his father's pants and shirt pockets, even if the pants were hanging in the closet. It was sort of mechanical by now, Samson went through the motions robotically. He was halfway through checking the pants, when his hand hit something unexpected. He was used to feeling nothing but fabric, but in a newly pressed pair of pants he touched something metallic. The simple fact that he touched anything at all surprised him so much he recoiled his hand quickly as if he touched a snake. His heart started beating wildly as he pushed his hand back in the pocket. It was something heavy and round, like a large coin.

Even though this revelation deflated him somewhat, because it wasn't the watch, he remained excited for some reason. He slowly pulled the large coin out of the pocket and he could not have been more surprised at what he held in his hand if it had been a full sized Tiger. He staggered in disbelieve, then dashed out of the room to show his sister what he found.

"Castilia, Castilia! You'll never guess what I found!" Samson said bounding into his sister's room as she lay in her bed with her casted foot raised up on a couple of pillow.

"You finally found that stupid watch you've been looking for for days," Castilia answered not looking up from the book she was reading.

"No, forget that, this is unbelievable!" Samson said too loudly. He was still bouncing around the room too excited to be still or quiet. Castilia looked up at him oddly, she felt queer. Her body was tingling slightly as if it has been asleep. She stared at her brother who was smiling so broadly his grin almost touched his ears. He look slightly maniacal. His excitement was infectious and she started to smile.

"OK, what is it? What could possibly get you this excited?" she sat up in her bed as much as she could.

Samson reached in his pocket, then suddenly paused and looked around to see if anyone was watching. He walked to the open door and shut it. When he turned around, he raised his hand to display a mildly glowing metal medallion. It was THE medallion. It had the wavy lines that crested into a swirls of water and spray that she now recognized so completely. It was the medallion from the Aquarium. Castilia was transfixed.

"Am I dreaming?" she said softly.

148

"No, it's the real deal." Samson said. "It glows hotter when I bring it close to mine." He brought the medallion closer to his chest and the glow intensified. Castilia could see Samson's medallion glowing beneath his shirt.

"But, how?... I mean, what?..." Castilia stammered.

"I know," Samson answered. "I have no idea. It was in Dad's pants pocket that just came back from the cleaners. It's a miracle."

"Can I hold it?" Castilia said meekly and held out her hand. Samson approached her and handed her the medallion.

When the medallion touched her skin there was a flash of light. Castilia let out a shrill scream and her hand grasped the medallion tightly, her knuckles turned white. She threw her head back on the pillow and closed her eyes. A fiery warmth shot up her arm and filled her body. She went rigid. It wasn't painful, but surprising. It actually felt good. The warmth filled her up like her blood was flowing through her body for the very first time. Her leg was burning up like it was on fire.

"Castilia!" Samson shouted and grabbed his sister's arms. "Castilia, are you ok?!" Samson didn't notice his smoldering shirt as the two medallions continued to glow incessantly.

Castilia's body relaxed and she let out a long, loud breath. The bright light of the two medallions began to fade. She slowly opened her eyes and smiled at her brother. "Never better." she said with a somber relaxed look in her eyes. "Wow, what a rush."

"What just happened?" Samson said, concerned, still holding on to his sister with a look of panic on his face as wafts of smoke from his shirt curled upwards around his head.

"I don't know but that felt great. My leg has stopped throbbing. Actually, it feels wonderful." She said in amazement and swung her legs over the edge of the bed. Before Samson could protest, she pushed him away and jumped to the floor and began dancing and twirling on her cast. "Oh my God! it doesn't hurt at all." She said in amazement.

"What are you doing? you're going to hurt yourself again." Samson scolded. Finally looking at his burnt shirt. "Crap, again?" he said under his breath.

"Can't you see? I'm fine, I'm healed. I knew this thing was magic. I just knew it. It's like it was meant to be mine, like I've been reunited with a long lost friend." She said now staring at the gray medallion in her hand.

"I know. That's exactly how I felt when granddad gave me this one. I don't remember it being such an explosive occasion, however." Samson said, looking down at his burnt shirt. "Mom's going to kill me again. I swear she thinks I'm smoking cigarettes. I'm going to have to throw this away."

"I don't know about you but I think it's time to take a walk up to the knoll," Castilia said with a wink and headed to her closet to get some clothes on.

Samson and Castilia ran into their Mom on the way out of the house.

"Just where do you think you are going? Did you finish your chores?" Mom said to Samson, not seeing her eldest daughter behind him. Samson's face fell into a look of despair.

"Mom." Castilia began, her mother jumped and smiled up at her daughter.

"Just what do you think you are doing out of bed, young lady?" Mom said surprised.

"I need to go outside, I'm getting so stir crazy. Samson said he would help me. I just need to lay in the grass and feel the sun on my face." Castilia answered and put a hand on Samson's shoulder as if he were supporting her.

"Oh, well..., that's very nice Samson. OK, take your sister out for a while, but you still need to finish your chores. Thisbe and Wylde are out there somewhere. They can help you too."

Brother and sister smiled at one another as Samson carefully helped his 'ailing' sister out the door.

Once out of sight of the back door and their mother's gaze, Samson and Castilia both started running toward the forest. This was particularly peculiar due to the fact Castilia was running at top speed with a full cast on her leg without any ill effect. Thisbe spotted this odd scene while lazily swinging on the old tire swing. She watched them hurry into the woods and then quickly and quietly jumped off the swing to follow them. Wylde was well into the woods poking a frog with a stick when he was surprised by the peculiar procession.

"Hey! where are you going?" he shouted not thinking anything of Castilia's reemergence into the wild. When he saw Thisbe running after them he took off in pursuit.

The chase ended at the large oak tree.

"What are you doing and how is Castilia running like a cheetah with a broken leg?" Thisbe asked, panting after the quick run.

Wylde skidded to a stop just as Thisbe asked this question. Samson and Castilia looked at each other and began laughing heartily.

"What's so funny?" Wylde asked still out of breath.

"I feel great!" Castilia said looking at Thisbe. "My leg seems to be all better because of this." She reached inside her shirt collar and pulled the newly found amulet out for Thisbe and Wylde to see.

"Where did you get THAT?" Wylde asked as Thisbe just stared with her mouth wide open.

Samson and Castilia sat down under the large oak in the shade and told their brother and sister about the events of the past hour. After they finished, the two new conspirators sat slack-jawed in front of them and didn't say a word. They both just looked incredulously at Castilia's amulet.

"So, Castilia was just healed? Just like that?" Wylde finally asked, still processing all that he was told.

"How did you get the amulet?" Thisbe asked before Samson or Castilia could answer Wylde's more important question.

Well, that's pretty much a mystery." Samson said again, relaying the information that he simply found the amulet in his Dad's newly-laundered clothes.

The discovery was quite serendipitous. Actually, it was more than that; it was downright improbable, but here it was, they had the amulet. On the night of the robbery the artifacts from the exhibit were taken from the case in the aquarium and moved to the back room for cleaning. This, of course, would take a few days, so the originals were replaced with replicas, as is common in such situations. The artifacts from that case had been scheduled for cleaning and restoration for quite some time. The staff had just not gotten around to doing it. That night, on the insistence of a low-level employee who felt a unnatural need to clean these items right away, the cleaning of the items were again brought to the attention of management. Given the motivation and moxie of the employee, the higher ups agreed and the items were placed on the back cleaning table for the impending task the next day, which had yet to be cleared from the last job. There were still soiled towels and cleaning rags laying about that had to be cleaned. The amulet in question was swept up by the cleaning crew with the old rags and dumped in the laundry bag to be sent out for cleaning. The cleaning company that did the maritime aquarium's laundry just so happened to be the very same laundry that did Mr. Presley's work pants and shirts on an irregular basis. Through the myriad of lucky coincidences, the amulet somehow landed in the pocket of Mr. Presley's pants.

"It's a mystery, but who cares!" Castilia continued excitedly. "We now have the amulet and it totally cured me! It's a miracle! I can't wait to get to the chamber and see what I can do."

"Wait a second, wait a second," Samson interrupted. "You think you're going to have some ability like me? Come on. What makes you think that."

"Are you kidding? You have the amulet and you can play with fire. Now I have a similar one AND it just cured me and you don't think I'll have some strange power too?" Castilia questioned.

"Oh, you're dreaming. You can't do what I can do. I'll admit that what just happened was strange, but I was thinking that I did that. If you think you'll have some power too, that's just wishful thinking." Samson said, not wanting to lose his exclusivity.

"You know, you really can be a self centered ass." Castilia said brusquely. "Let's just find the opening and see." and she quickly began stomping around looking for the chamber door.

"Thunk!" Wylde found it immediately just under the spot where he was standing listening to his brother and sister argue.

They quickly uncovered the door and dropped the ladder down into the chamber.

Almost immediately, Samson lit up the place with a fireball that consumed his hand.

"Totally cool," he said, as he waved his hand around the space in flames.

Castilia slowly descended the ladder, anticipating some cosmic epiphany to jolt her to her new superhero persona. She felt good, but nothing changed as she lowered herself rung by rung. She felt completely normal as her foot and cast hit the wet pool at the bottom of the ladder.

"Humm...nothing's happening." she said to herself as she jumped out of the pool and watched Samson running around in circles with his hands alight like a sparkler. He was waving his hands around in the air with a stupid grin on his face in complete glee. He could really be a complete moron sometimes.

"Maybe I should be in front of my mural." she thought to herself, so she made her way to the corner of the chamber that depicted images of water. She looked around pensively and quietly snapped her fingers.

Still, nothing.

Castilia picked up the amulet around her neck and looked at it curiously. It seemed heavy and useless, just a stupid piece of metallic junk. It wasn't glowing or anything.

Samson ran by. His whole right arm was ablaze and he was showering sparks over Wylde's head. "Anything yet?" he said grinning like a Cheshire Cat at Castilia.

"No..." she said pensively. "Nothing yet."

Samson continued to run around the chamber sparking and flaming much to the delight of himself and Wylde. This went on for what seemed like an eternity to Castilia as she tried everything she knew to do. She thought real hard for a while, she screamed, she snapped, clapped, danced, stomped and jumped. Nothing. She dropped to the ground dejected. Thisbe walked over to her sister, sat down, and put her arm around her shoulders.

Thisbe whispered into Castilia's ear, "Perhaps it's not time."

Castilia started crying uncontrollably. She was sobbing hysterically until Samson stopped in his tracks and looked at her with pity.

"Hey, I didn't mean anything...I mean I didn't want to upset you..." he stuttered at Castilia.

"Here..." Samson said and pushed his hand toward her sister, who was still sobbing. "Look at this, I made this for you."

"Wow, that's beautiful." Thisbe said staring at Samson's hand.

Castilia opened her eyes to see a fiery rose levitating just above Samson's outstretched hand. She looked up to her brother who was staring into her eyes and said "Thanks. That's nice."

After that, nothing untoward happened to Castilia, but she continued to be in tune with her body and constantly checked the amulet during that visit. Samson, however, seemed to flourish during the chamber visit. He was able to turn on and off the fire at will and didn't have to use the "snap" to do it. He was able to control how far up his arm the fire went and even began to make shapes with the fire in his hand as evidenced by the rose for Castilia.

They of course ended up staying much longer than they intended and were interrupted by the Presley dinner bell clanging loudly up above.

"Great, I'm starving!" Wylde said as he quickly ascended the ladder.

They all suddenly discovered they were just as famished and followed their brother up and out of the oculus.

"Well, I guess it's not my time," Castilia said to Samson as they both climbed out of the door.

"What do you know anyway," Samson said shortly, "you may never have a time."

"Have I mentioned how great of a brother your are." Castilia curtly said.

"No, as a matter of fact you haven't," he said as the grin returned to his face.

"Good. You need to remember to help me into the house, so don't go sprinting off," Castilia reminded him as they shut the heavy wooden door.

They all headed to the house in the late afternoon sun. A while after the four siblings had left the knoll a tall dark figure slowly crept up to the spot from which they crawled out of the ground. It surveyed the site and walked around in circles looking at the bare ground. It kicked the ground with it's foot, moving dirt and leaves around. It clearly didn't find what it was looking for and stood with its hands on its hips for a while looking here and there. It then slowly slipped back down the knoll as the sun set and darkness began to set in.

CHAPTER 21

The Campout

Castilia tried her best to show a gradual improvement with her leg over the next few days but was continually caught by her mother running or jumping around as if nothing was wrong. This charade continued until her Mother spotted her chasing Wylde at full speed across the yard as Wylde was waving her favorite new shirt in the air behind him. A doctor's appointment was made at this point and her cast was removed after the x-ray revealed her bone had completely healed. The doctors were perplexed. They ran a full day's worth of test on her leg until they seemed to be satisfied that there was simply nothing wrong with her. They released her scratching their heads.

Samson continued his half-hearted watch search for another few days until one morning his mother proposed a deal for him. Mr. Finch had invited Samson and his dad out for a weekend camping trip. If Samson would go without any whining or complaining, they would lift the watch-induced punishment. Because the last encounter with Argus was not completely horrendous, and, in fact was quite enjoyable, Samson decided a couple of days with Argus was definitely better than the continued pain of nonsensically searching for something that clearly was not there. He agreed to the condition.

Also that morning, Dad read in the newspaper that the Maritime Aquarium reported that the items stolen a couple of weeks ago turned out to be replicas of the originals that had been replaced that afternoon for cleaning. "The thieves made off with nothing more than a few fake items," Dad reported with a laugh. "It does say here that while most of the items will be back in the exhibit next week. One of the pieces has gone missing."

Castilia looked at Samson with a sly grin.

Samson decided to celebrate his release from his incarceration with a trip into town after lunch for some ice cream and possibly a video game or two. "Ice cream is on me!" Samson declared to cheers by all. So they gathered their bikes to join in Samson's newly-regained freedom.

Once downtown they parked their bikes and headed toward the ice cream shop for their treat and noticed someone pacing back and forth on the sidewalk wringing his hands and looking clearly distraught.

"Is that... Dr. Lovejoy?" Castilia asked.

"Are you kidding, Dr. Lovejoy would never look like..." Samson stopped talking and looked hard down the sidewalk. "I think you're right. Maybe we should go help him." They all headed toward Dr. Lovejoy. As they approached, they saw he was clearly not himself. His usually quaffed hair was unruly and out of sorts. His white suit was soiled and he was not clean shaven. As they got closer they could see bags under his bloodshot eyes and heard him muttering, "It's not the right one...she's going to be very angry...Got to find it..."

"D-D-Dr. Lovejoy?" Castilia said with concern. "Are you alright?"

This startled Dr. Lovejoy, and he turned and stared at them with empty, fearful eyes. Almost immediately, recognition hit his face and he straightened up and closed his eyes as his hands flew up to smooth his hair. When he looked back at them his eyes had regained their usual luster and his big smile appeared.

"Ahhh... Hello there Presleys..." he began in his smooth confident voice, looking at each of them, then looking down at himself , "Please excuse my appearance, I, uh, I've, uh... I've been up all night, uh. Looking... um. Yes, looking for... Mrs. Sander's dog." He paused, clearly regaining his composure now. "Poor thing's gotten itself lost and the dear lady is beside herself. If you'll excuse me, I need to take care of a few things." He bowed and quickly retreated down the street, leaving the kids staring after him.

"That was weird," Wylde said. "I've always thought there was something off about that guy... Oh well, how about that ice cream?," he said turning to Samson as they both headed to the Ice Cream Shop.

"Definitely weird," Castilia said to Thisbe thoughtfully. "Did you hear what he was saying? He was clearly frightened. There's more to this than a lost dog, I'm pretty sure." The sisters slowly turned and followed their brothers to get their promised treat.

* * *

The next weekend the family all had plans away from Westville. Mom was taking the girls for an overnight trip into the city. Wylde had a sleepover at a friend from Adventure Camp's house a couple of towns away. Samson and his father packed up the camping gear and headed out toward the Housatonic River Valley for a two-day camping trip. They would hike in Saturday morning and camp over night, and then leave the next day. It was going to be a hot weekend so Dad picked an easy three to four mile hike in with camping near the river so they could play and cool off as required. They met the Finchs at the trail head. As an archeologist, Professor Finch was not necessarily used to hiking into a camp, as much as driving into a camp and therefore had an absurd amount of camping gear including a wooden table and chairs. It took about an hour for Dad to sort through the stuff and get the packs for the Finchs down to a more suitable weight for the hike in. In the mean-time, Argus and Samson decided to pass the time finding frogs and crayfish in the small brook that flowed by the parking area. It was clear to Samson that Argus could be nice at times but had a demented sense of humor and a troubling sadistic bent. The first frog he found he threw it at Samson's head, which was painful enough for Samson, but the frog, after tumbling back down on the rocks, was severely injured.

"Hey!" Samson said after getting smacked in the head with the wet frog. "What the heck are you doing?!"

"What? That was funny!" Argus said, laughing.

"Not to the frog," Samson pointed out angrily. "I think you broke its leg."

"It's just a frog - a raccoon will eat it later," Argus said, dismissing Samson and looking around for more frogs.

"Listen, I don't care what you do to me, but lets just leave the animals out of it from now on." Samson said, glaring at Argus.

"Ok, ok. I didn't realize you were so sensitive." Argus said as Samson turned his back on him to check on the wounded frog. Smack! Something wet and smelly hit the back of Samson's neck. He almost fell into the stream, but caught himself by splashing both hands in the cool shallow water. He raised his left hand to his head to find a mixture of wet leaves, mud and moss.

"Is that better?" Argus said as he began to laugh. Samson was boiling. He grasped a clump of mud and leaves in his right hand as he quickly rose and hurled the debris as hard as he could at Argus - hitting him square in the face.

"Yes, much." Samson said with a smug look on his face while Argus spit mud from his mouth and wiped it away from his eyes. Samson braced himself for the reprisal. He was tense but didn't much care what happened at this point - that was definitely worth it. Argus looked at him with a twisted surprised face and started laughing hysterically.

"Now that's more like it!" he bellowed. "Nice shot! I even think you got some up my nose!" He blew dirt out of his nose and continued laughing.

Samson, still a bit confused and tense, laughed lightly at first, not sure if this was a trick and unwilling to put his guard down just yet.

"No one ever does that to me. That was awesome!" Argus was laughing so hard that he slipped and fell into the muddy brook. At this Samson relaxed and began laughing at the ridiculous situation. Argus was totally filthy at this point and began half-heartedly throwing mud in Samson's direction, which he easily avoided, however, he wasn't able to avoid losing his balance and falling into the water just like Argus had done moments before. After a few more minutes, they were both covered from head to foot with mud, leaves and twigs, looking like some kind of dirty Yeti. They sloshed back to the car as their fathers had just managed to get everything packed up.

"Oh my God. What have you two gotten into?" Professor Finch asked in disbelief.

"Looks like we might want to unpack some fresh clothes for the hike, unless the two mudfish want to get a nice rash on the way in." Dad said laughing.

The hike was easy enough, even with the fairly heavy packs they each had. They made it to the camp site in no time and began to set up camp. It was a nice, fairly flat grass clearing a short way from the river. It was quiet and serene. All that could be heard was the gentle gurgle of the river beyond. After setting up camp and gathering enough fire wood to fuel a funeral pyre, they spent the rest of the afternoon cooling off in the river. There was a high rope swing in an old oak tree dangling over the water a few yards upstream. Even Professor Finch gave it a go. The four boys had a grand time. After a well crafted camp meal, they all gathered around the camp fire to talk and get ready for bed.

"That was a fun day boys," Dad said rubbing his belly as he dropped down on the grass by the fire. "I hope you enjoyed it as much as I did. I have to say I'm about worn out," he said with a yawn. The other three followed his lead and found a comfortable spot to stretch out around the fire.

"It was, indeed, a joyful experience. Thank you so much for taking the time to come with us. And of course finding this wonderful spot." Professor Finch added. The sky was glowing pink from the setting of the sun and the air cooled considerably. The fire felt nice in the crisp mountain air. It crackled and sparked as the four sat contented, gazing at the flames.

Samson had been thinking for a while chewing on a piece of grass in the comfortable silence and spoke up after a few moments, "Professor Finch, I've been meaning to ask you about something."

"Please do, my boy. I am at your disposal." Proessor. Finch said with a wink.

"About a month back, my sister heard a lecture you gave at the Peabody Museum about the four elements. She came back and told us about it, but she said you were very vague about the whole thing. Why is that?" Samson asked.

"Oh, here we go..." Argus said, rolling his eyes. "Don't get him started. He'll never stop."

"Hush, Argus. The boy asked me a legitimate and curious question. The answer, however, is going to be disappointing. The simple truth is that there is not much there. While every culture and religion has mentioned the four elements in some form or another, there does not seem to be very much other than the basics. It's curious that something that is so universal did not develop into a religion of its own. The legend, however, of the elements is so old, that perhaps, there was a form of religion before written history. I've written many books on the subject, but most of them are based on conjecture. There are very few hard facts on the subject - mostly just old stories and rumors. However I strongly believe the elements are the key to life as we know it. I'm afraid that not too many people give my theories any credence. Regardless, it is a fascinating subject and I'm glad you show some interest in it."

Samson though about this for a minute and asked, "But you also mentioned that there were some artifacts associated with the elements. What are those?"

"Boring! Can't we tell some ghost stories or something?" Argus interrupted loudly.

"Haha, perhaps I can kill two birds with one stone my dear son." Professor Finch answered as Samson glared at Argus for the rude outburst. "There is a pre-historic legend that may be just what everyone needs. It is mostly a verbal history that I've put together combining stories from ancient civilizations spanning the Fertile Crescent to Mayan Cultures in Latin America. I've taken liberties with some of the translations, but it seems to encompass the meaning of the legend fairly well I think. Would you like to hear it?"

"Sure." Samson said, not sure if his question was going to get answered or not. Dad looked tired lying by the fire, but gave a lazy nod of accent.

"I guess so," Argus added, sounding bored.

"Well then, it's unanimous." Professor Finch looked up at the stars as he gathered his thoughts.

"In the beginning there was only one human tribe called the Ni. They lived in harmony with the land and with each other for millennia. The Ni were respectful of each other and there was no real leader or group of authority. Older generations passed their knowledge to the younger ones as they came of age. There was no hierarchy other than love, respect and age. Over time four siblings, two brothers and two sisters, became known as the four great bears because of their domineering personalities and physical strength. They were called Conze, Wisosoka, Ahoicope and Inawizi. This roughly translates to Wrath, Greed, Pride and Envy, which, of course, is another coincidence that cannot be overlooked."

"Why is that a coincidence?" Samson interrupted.

"Oh, excuse me, my boy, sometimes I assume too much. Wrath, Greed, Pride and Envy are 4 of Dante's seven deadly sins of Christian ethics, you see. Which in my mind are the most heinous of the lot. So these four siblings became..."

"So what are the other three?" Samson interrupted again.

"Excuse me?..Three, three what?" Professor Finch asked confused at Samson's question.

"The other three deadly sins. You said there were seven." Samson clarified.

"Sloth, Lust and Gluttony. Jeesh, just get on with it." Argus said quickly and folded his arms impatiently. Samson stared at Argus in amazement. This boy was full of surprises.

"Quite right, quite right, Argus. Now were was I?.. Oh yes, The four siblings - two brothers and two sisters - became anxious and restless with their elders as they wanted to know the ancient secrets of the tribe. They pushed and harassed the elders until they relinquished their knowledge. Even then they were not satisfied with what they were told. They thought something was being held back from them. They were searching for rules of power, not balance, and the elders had no knowledge of such things. They began to raid other communities of the Ni and put the elders into servitude until they too told their secrets. As time ran on the four gained more power and through this power always strove to obtain more. They began a rule of force and enslavement. As it is told, this is when man first held dominion over the beasts. Before the four great bears, man and beasts were one. The four great bears threw the world out of balance and a reign of terror began. After years of fighting the Ni, the four great bears began to fight amongst themselves and became envious and mistrusted one another. The Ni fractured into 4 distinct groups led by each of the siblings. War was ongoing.

The last of the Ni knew that they must bring balance back to the world by pulling strength from the very origins of all things - the four elements: Earth, Water, Wind and Fire. They used the elements to harness natures's power and created four talismans to capture and focus that power. The talismans were forged of earth by fire, molded by wind, and cooled and tempered by water.

The last of the Ni found four siblings that were true of heart to become the vessels of the elements and champions of the talismans. They were Makoce, Mni, Tate and Peta. The new warriors were given great power through the talismans and then were sent to destroy the great bears. They won many battles against the separate tribes and the tribes became fractured and weak. The great bears, however, afraid of losing the power they so loved, banded together to defeat the elements. Indeed their strength together was no match for the four champions. An epic battle ensued and the four champions were on the brink of destruction. The great bears brought them to the most sacred Ni mountain to destroy them once and for all and end the realm of the Ni. It was then that Wisosoka (Greed) stole the talismans from the champions as she wanted the power for herself. Conze (Wrath) and Inawizi (Envy) soon discovered they had been betrayed by their sister and attacked her in a fury. Ahoicope

(Pride) watched as her siblings fought and was able to gather the talismans in the confusion. She used the power of the talisman to mortally wound the other great bears and stood alone at the top of the world, now drunk with power. Ahoicope no longer considered the four champions to be a threat; however, the four champions, in this most desperate hour, came together and created the Iyuha, or what I like to call the fifth element. The fifth element was a power stronger than anything ever known and it struck down Ahoicope and covered the world. When it receded, the great bears were no more and balance was restored. It is said that the stars are rips in the sky caused by the Iyuha. Things did not, however, return back as they were with Ni. The four tribes remained split and settled different parts of the earth and dominion over the beasts remained. I assume the four tribes are some form of European, Asian, African and American extraction. After the Iyuha, the four champions were legend and ruled the four tribes peacefully for centuries. The talismans became sacred symbols to remind the tribes of the balance of nature and the threat of the four bears."

"So what happened to them? What happened to the talismans? And what is the Iyuha?" Samson asked, anxious to know more.

"Those are two great questions. I've been trying to answer both of them for years. That story was handed down for centuries, but it does not end there. Legend has it that the following of the great bears continued even after their defeat and became known as the Hehatu. They re-emerge at times of moral weakness to once again regain power. Each time, the four champions returned to banish the Hehatu back to darkness and restore balance. Perhaps it is just a legend and no such things exist.

Perhaps it is just symbolism for something else entirely. I do find it hard to believe that so many cultures can include this same symbolism in their respective belief systems for this not to have some shred of truth," Professor Finch finished, gazing longingly at the stars above his head.

"That story sucked," Argus said belligerently. "I could tell a better ghost story when I was five years old." Professor Finch glared over at Argus and opened his mouth for an admonition, thought better of it, and laid his head back down with a sigh and closed his eyes.

"I thought it was excellent." Samson retorted in defense of Professor Finch. He had so many questions he wanted to ask.

"Well, that's because you are a wuss. Now here's a good ghost story," Argus rubbed his hands together, cleared his throat began. "I heard this REALLY happened. Not too far from here actually. It was a dark and stormy night. A middle-aged man, his name was Alfred, was driving down a dark highway and his headlights caught a thin young woman in a white dress and blonde hair standing gloomily by the road. She lazily flagged him down. The driver asked what a pretty girl like her was doing on a dark highway like this..." Argus continued his story but Samson was not listening. He was rubbing his medallion under his shirt, looking at the tears in the night sky and wondering.

There was no more talk of the Elements the next morning as everyone prepared a hearty breakfast and then began to break down the camp. Dad had to get back fairly early so everything got packed up and they began the hike back out. Argus seemed to be getting fairly comfortable with Samson and continued to act like a semi-normal human being. Samson's impression of Argus had definitely changed. However, Argus was still too unpredictable. Samson was not yet ready to let his guard down completely.

CHAPTER 22

The Break In

The ride back was uneventful and Samson and his Dad were the first of the family to return to Fox Hollow. The girls wouldn't be back until well after lunch ,and Wylde even later. Dad grabbed a load of things to carry into the house. Samson did the same, following his fathers lead toward the house, when his Dad stopped abruptly, causing him to run into him and drop the load he was carrying. A sleeping bag, pots and pans, and a lantern crashed on the ground.

"Hey!" Samson said looking at the mess. "What are you do..." Samson looked to see his father slowing putting down items he had in his hands and staring at the front of the house. Then he saw what his Dad was looking at. One of the dogs was laying in a pool of blood at the top of the stairs by the front door. Flies were buzzing around the still body. The front door was open slightly. The other dogs were nowhere to be seen, which was unusual as they were all typically under your heels when you stepped out of the car. Samson started to run toward the dog but his father stopped him.

"We don't know if someone is still here. Run over to the neighbors house and call the police. My cell phone is dead. I'm going to get my gun out of the barn." Dad whispered looking warily at his son.

Samson turned to go but stopped when something odd occurred to him, "You've got a gun in the barn?" he asked.

"Never mind that now, go call the police," Dad said in a stern voice and pushed him down the drive as he moved cautiously toward the barn while keeping his eyes on the house.

Samson backed away slowly until he reached the edge of the parking area, then turned and ran as fast as he could to the neighbors house which was a quarter mile away through the adjoining woods.

He burst into the Valentine's yard and saw Mr. Valentine immediately working in his vegetable garden with his large straw hat.

"CALL 911, CALL 911!" Samson screamed as he continued to run toward his neighbor.

Mr. Valentine was a very large man with short cropped red hair and fair skin that remained pink during the summer season. He and his wife were a bit older than Mom and Dad and their kids were all in or finished with college.

"What is it, Samson! What's the matter?" He turned immediately and started toward Samson.

"We just got back and someone's in the house. They killed Pony." Samson said frantically.

"Where's your father?," Mr. Valentine demanded quickly.

"He's watching the house and sent me here to call the police." Samson answered.

"Run in the house and use the phone, Mrs. Valentine is in there, Stay here in the house and wait for your father to come and get you. Hurry!" he said. As Samson ran to the house, Mr. Valentine picked up his pitchfork and ran back the way Samson came.

Samson made the call and was very anxious. Mrs. Valentine was not able to calm him down. Remarkably soon after the 911 call, Samson heard the sirens screaming down the road. He raced to the door and saw the blue and red lights flashing through the trees. Mrs. Valentine was no longer able to restrain him and he burst out of the door and raced back toward home with Mrs. Valentine yelling out of the door, "Samson, come back!" Quickly realizing that was futile she added, "You stay clear of the house! Don't get too close!"

Samson sped toward the house and only slowed as he came to the edge of the woods at the driveway. He could see the police cars at the house and his father talking animatedly to one of the officers. Mr. Valentine was standing nearby leaning on his pitchfork listening to the conversation. Samson crept slowly forward toward his father.

"I don't know," Samson heard his father saying. "We were all gone last night and the house was locked and the alarm was on. When we got back this morning we found Pony on the porch and the door ajar."

An officer approached from the house. "The house is all clear, Sir. It is quite a mess. Would you mind coming in and doing a quick survey for us. See what is missing?"

Dad noticed Samson slowly approaching with a panicked face. "It's all right, Samson," he said giving him a hug. "Go check on the other animals and see if you can locate the other dogs while I take a look around inside."

"Dad I want to go with you." Samson was quite shaken.

"Let me check it out first. I'm sure it will give us both peace of mind to know the rest of the animals are OK. Go check them out and wait on the porch for me to come out."

"Sam, I'm so sorry I didn't hear anything last night. Please let me know if there's anything we can do." Mr. Valentine said as he turned to go. "I'd better get back home before Carol get's too worried."

"Thanks for coming over Ken." Dad nodded.

Samson did a quick run around the property. He found the other two dogs hiding under the back porch and coaxed them out after a good bit of verbal reassurance. The chickens were in their run, unaffected by what had happened at the house. Samson headed back and waited on the porch for what seemed like an eternity as police officers streamed in and out. Finally, his father stepped out of the front door scratching his head looking out at the front yard for a while until he noticed Samson standing patiently to the side and looking forlorn.

"There you are," his Dad said with a smile, "Come on in. They definitely made a mess but nothing seems to be missing. Damnedest thing. See if you notice anything."

Samson headed inside following his father. The house had been ransacked. Cushions, books, newspapers, coats and hats, pots and pans, mail and miscellaneous things littered the floor. Samson was amazed that his Dad was even able to tell that nothing was missing. He quickly ran upstairs to his room. It was a mess. All of the drawers were open with clothes thrown on every surface. The beds had been tossed and pillows and sheets thrown around the room. The closet door was wide open and clothes hung roughshod on the hangers. Even the window shades were pulled down at strange angles. Samson stood gapping at the mess when his Dad came up behind him.

"Yep, it's amazing," he said, "They messed up every room in the house but your room looks just like you left it."

Samson turned to his father who was stifling a grin and then suddenly burst out into a loud hearty laugh. Samson started laughing too. It was and awkward laugh but helped them deal with the absurdity of the situation. It quickly came to an end but made them both feel better. "This is totally not funny. I'm glad your mother isn't here." Dad said.

They continued their survey of the second floor. All of the rooms were the same, completely tossed, but everything was accounted for, as far as they could tell in the mess. They both reported to the police that couldn't see anything of value that was missing at present but would begin a clean up and see what came up. In the meantime, the police found a large scrap of black fabric in Pony's mouth. It looked as if the brave dog had tried to stop the intruders before he was stabbed by the perpetrator and bled out on the porch.

"I hope he took a chunk out of the bastard's leg." Samson said to himself.

For a few hours the house was a real crime scene - they took pictures and dusted for prints, made diagrams, measured, made copies of shoe prints and took notes. The police said they would write up a report and have them come in again after they had a chance to clean up and assess the damage. Samson and his father showed the police to the door and watched them leave. Once back outside, the reality of the deceased dog hit them both.

"We need to take care of Pony first. Go get a couple of shovels and let's find a suitable burial plot. Let's try and get this done before the girls get home. Your Mother is going to be terribly upset." Dad said.

They found a nice spot at the far end of the yard under a large shade tree that Pony used to spend his days sleeping and buried him there. They decided they would have a family ceremony that evening. They then trudged back to the house to begin the cleanup. It wasn't long before Mom and the girls got back. Luckily, Samson had just finished cleaning the blood off of the front porch. Mom was immediately hysterical and it took a while for her to calm down. Dad discussed what had happened with Mom in the kitchen. The girls didn't seem to be too upset, but got the lowdown from Samson out on the porch and went out to visit Pony's grave. That made Thisbe very sad and she cried for a long time under the tree, the wind blowing in her hair.

When Wylde finally returned, they all gathered under the tree to pay their last respects to their devoted dog as the sun began to set.

"Pony was a good dog." Dad eulogized. "He didn't ask for much. Only for a nice bone and a good scratch between the ears every now and again. He had a heart of gold and was always happy to see you. We learned today that the world can be a savage place, but there are a few brave souls that will stand up in the face of evil and sacrifice themselves for what they know is right. Pony was one of those. We should all strive to be so good. May he live forever in peace in our hearts."

That night in the house was a restless one for everyone but Wylde who could sleep through a hurricane. The others spent hours moving from room to room until they all decided to set up camp on the floor in their parents room. They finally fell asleep in the wee hours of the morning. This house that had once seemed like a fortress, now didn't seem safe at all.

CHAPTER 23

The Hospital Again

As word spread of the break-in, friends came by to make sure everyone was OK and to offer any help they could give. Everything slowly found its way back into its place and the house became a home again. The police found no usable fingerprints and had no motive or leads in the case. After the clean up, Mom and Dad confirmed that nothing was stolen. The worst that happened was that a few decorative porcelain items had broken when thrown to the floor. Most people who came by said they had been lucky, but no one really felt lucky.

Dr. Lovejoy stopped by and had tea with Mom and briefly chatted with the kids and encouraged them to "Trust in the Lord, as he works in mysterious ways."

"This didn't seem very mysterious, just wantonly intrusive." Castilia replied, annoyed at the platitude. Mom glared disapprovingly at Castilia as Dr. Lovejoy laughed it off and said his goodbyes.

"We need to go see Mrs. Goodwyn again. These "dark figures" may be more dangerous than she let on." Samson suggested. "Plus I'd like to ask her about the legend Professor Finch told me on the camping trip." Samson had relayed the story of the great bears to his brother and sisters the night of the break-in, which could also have contributed to their wakefulness that night.

"I think that is a great idea," Thisbe said and ran to the phone to give Mrs. Goodwyn a call. "No one answered," she said when she returned. "She didn't even have an answering machine."

"How can she not have an answering machine?" Samson said in frustration. "I guess you'll just have to try again later."

Mom said she needed to get out of the house they had been straightening up the last few days and took everyone to the pool. Castilia was very grateful for the trip. She had not been in the water since she had her accident. She was in desperate need to swim some laps which she proceeded to do the entire time they were there. The rest of the crew spent their time splashing around and diving off the diving board and generally having fun in the cool water and not thinking of the events of the past few days.

By the time the weekend rolled in again, and Thisbe had called Mrs. Goodwyn several times to no avail, they decided to visit the historical society and ask Mrs. Grumman, the librarian, if Mrs. Goodwyn was out of town or something. So they all donned their helmets and headed to town on their bikes.

They made it to the Historical Society in no time, but this time Samson, Castilia and Wylde didn't even attempt to go inside as they were all hot, dirty and sweaty. All except for Thisbe, who bounded off her bike and quickly glided up the stairs into the library. A few moments later, Thisbe appeared at the entry door with her head in her hands weeping hysterically.

Samson jumped off his bike to help her down the stairs. It took a while to calm her down and finally discover what has upset her so. Mrs. Goodwyn had been in the hospital for the last week and her daughter had taken off work to be there with her. Mrs. Cornblatt, the greeter, did not know what had happened. The kids walked their bikes across the park to the ice cream store to get something to eat and a cool drink and think about what to do next. Thisbe was insistent that they go visit Mrs. Goodwyn in the hospital and wouldn't let the discussion venture to another topic. So it was decided. They finished their ice creams in silence and then rode home to find their mother.

Mom was shaken by the news. Thisbe picked a bouquet of wildflowers and then they all piled into the van and headed for the hospital.

The hospital visit was a bit unnerving as it had been way too recent since their last visit with Castilia. Thisbe got a chill when she walked in. They found their way to Mrs. Goodwyn's room easy enough and lightly knocked on the door.

"Come in," said a quiet voice.

As they slowly opened the door they saw Mrs. Grumman in the chair by the bed with an open book in her lap. Mrs. Goodwyn lay in the bed and looked as old as she had on their first visit. She had very little color in her face, her hair was unkempt, and her eyes were closed. An IV line dangled down to her left arm and the familiar ping of the heart monitor echoed in the room. She looked like Death was knocking at her door. Mrs. Grumman quietly laid the book on the bedside table and stood up to greet the guests, she too looked tired and old.

"Is she...is she sleeping?" Castilia asked softly, looking apprehensively towards Mrs. Goodwyn. Before Mrs. Grumman could answer, her mother stirred and said,"No, child. I'm not sleeping. I was just pretending so my daughter would stop reading me that god-awful book she brought in to pass the time." Mrs. Goodwyn smiled and opened her eyes.

"Mother," Mrs. Grumman chastized, "Just tell me you don't like it."

"Well, you seemed to be enjoying it." Mrs. Goodwyn answered. "Now, how are my favorite children?"

"Never mind that, how are you?" Samson stepped forward to her bed and everyone followed.

"I'm old. That's the only thing wrong with me." Mrs. Goodwyn said, and looked at her daughter with a frown. At that, Mom offered to buy Mrs. Grumman a coffee and they left the room.

"I kept telling them my insides are old and dusty and that seems to be the final prognosis." Mrs. Goodwyn said. "However, they still won't let me out of here for some unknown reason."

"What happened to get you in here?" Wylde asked.

"That is a good question, Wylde, and I think the answer is 'not much.' I guess I fainted and fell across the coffee table, which gave my daughter quite the scare. She was convinced that I broke my hip or something. I was up late Saturday night as I am apt to do because I often take wonderful naps during the day. I had gotten a cup of tea from the kitchen and was making my way back to my bedroom when all of a sudden, something took my breath away. Next thing I knew I woke up in an ambulance and they have poked and prodded me ever since. Now here I am in this hospital bed."

"So are you going to be all right?" Thisbe asked her voice quivering.

"It is not yet my time, dear." Mrs. Goodwyn answered and gently put her hand to Thisbe's cheek and wiped away a tear. "I'm very grateful you came to visit. So please, tell me how you are."

"A lot has happened to us since we last met, beginning immediately after I ran out of your house that day." Castilia began. They all told Mrs. Goodwyn about the accident, the cast and the new talisman, the story of the great bears and then the break in. Mrs. Goodwyn listened patiently as they took turns filling in the story.

"And someone broke into your house and killed your dog on Saturday night?" Mrs. Goodwyn asked after they had finished.

"That's right," Samson confirmed.

"That makes more sense, then," Mrs. Goodwyn said, and stared up at the ceiling for a while as the kids looked at each other and patiently waited for her to come back to them. She suddenly shuttered and looked at each of them with fear in her eyes. "Things are going to get worse before they get better I'm afraid...They seem to know you are special and are focusing more of their energy on you. I don't think they know why."

"What do they want? Why did they kill Pony?" Castilia asked.

"What do they always want? Power, money...Money and Power. Killing Pony was probably an accident but it shows that they are ruthless. They do not yet seem to be desperate. When that happens, there will be real trouble." Mrs. Goodwyn said with an air of urgency that sent chills through the children.

"What should we do?," Samson asked.

"That is not clear. I think what you are doing is what you should do. I do not get the sense that anything is going wrong." Mrs. Goodwyn said.

"What?!!" Castilia was getting worked up again. "Someone ran over me with a car and our dog is dead! That seems really wrong to me." Samson put his hand on her shoulder and gave her a look to calm her down.

"That indeed is true, my dear, but you do have the other talisman which seemed to be an almost impossible stroke of good luck." Mrs. Goodwyn calmly retorted.

"But you said the talismans were not important." Castilia reminded her.

"No, I said I did not see the importance of the talismans. That is a completely different notion." Turning to Samson, Mrs. Goodwyn placed her hand on his and continued, "You will have to make an important decision soon. It will alter your life. Choose wisely and be true to yourself."

"Ugh, Are you kidding? That's not fair at all," Samson said, pulling his hand away and sulking. "How am I supposed to know how to choose wisely. I hardly ever choose wisely...with anything. In fact, I'm known for making very unwise decisions."

"It's true," Castilia smirked, "he does make poor decisions."

"Samson, you will look into your heart and do what you think it right. This is not a choice between selecting a candy bar or a piece of fruit for your snack. This is a choice that will impact others and, in turn, yourself. You have a good heart. I see it in your interactions with your brother and sisters - you have nothing to fear." Mrs. Goodwyn smiled gently at him and he felt much better. Mrs. Goodwyn closed her eyes for a long moment. "Your visit was much appreciated and very welcome, but I'm afraid I need my rest if I'm ever going to get out of here. Thank you so much for coming. I hope to see you again soon... at home," she said with a wink.

Everyone said their goodbyes and gave Mrs. Goodwyn well wishes and then left her room in search of their mother.

CHAPTER 24

Captain McKain

Samson had a fairly boring time the following week as everyone was busy doing this and that. Thisbe and Castilia had several playdates and sleepovers with friends who had come back from vacation. Wylde was busy at a summer soccer league. This left Samson with not much to do but fish and avoid his mother, in case she got any ideas about giving him more chores to do. He had learned a couple of years ago to never tell his parents he was bored or had nothing to do. This admission always brought about a flurry of chores. He found it much easier to get lost out in the woods and go fishing or find frogs or snakes or just lounge about by the river. The woods were always full of surprises and he was always curious to discover some new insect, bird or animal living nearby. This week, however, brought a couple of unexpected surprises outside of the woods.

Around mid week, Samson rode his bike up to town and heard someone call his name.

"Samson!" Argus Finch called out when he spotted Samson riding his bike down the street. Samson spun around and rode up to Argus who was leaning smugly against the lamp post on the sidewalk looking as if he didn't have a care in the world.

"Hey," Samson said as he came to a stop in front of Argus, "What are you doing here?"

"Oh, my Dad's just picking up some things at the grocery and didn't want me to bother him so I'm waiting out here." Argus said, with a little shrug of his shoulders. "Hey, what are you doing next week? Like on Wednesday?"

"Probably the same thing I'm doing today. Absolutely nothing. Why?" Samson answered curiously.

"Listen, keep this on the down low, but I'm working on something epic for next week. It will involve sneaking out of the house at midnight. Are you in?" Argus asked, eyeing Samson for any sign of weakness or being girly.

"I don't know, Argus. I don't think I can sneak out of our house. I'm not even sure my Mom ever sleeps. Anytime any of us even cough at night, she's instantly hovering over our beds, feeling our foreheads; plus the house is old and creaky. I'd be busted before I even got out of the door." Samson said, trying not to sound like too much of a wuss.

"I can sneak out of my house easy. Dad snores like a chain-saw all night. I think I could drive a truck through the house and he would never wake up." Argus began. "What if I invite you to spend the night and we could do it then."

"I don't know Argus, it seems pretty risky. I don't think we should be sneaking out of the house." Argus gave Samson a sneer. Samson knew he was sounding like a wuss now and braced himself for what was coming next.

"Oh, come on! Are you going to be a girl all of your life?" Argus was just getting started. "This is a perfect opportunity for you to have some fun. It's going to be epic, I assure you. Don't be such a baby. It's not even fun unless you're not supposed to do it. Had I known you were such a goody two shoes, I never would have brought it up."

"OK, OK." Samson said. Argus had called him a girl, a baby and a goody two shoes within ten seconds. Samson really had no recourse other than to quickly agree to go along or things were going to get ugly. Next came the cursing, then the shouting, then very possibly, the beating. He definitely didn't want to go there, and besides, how bad could a sleepover with Argus be? Samson had a good time on the camping trip. "You'll have to have your father set it up with my Mom."

"Cool, it will be great!" Argus said relaxing now that he didn't have to ramp up his rhetoric.

"So what exactly are you planning? Or do I want to know?" Samson asked hesitantly.

"They'll be talking about it for months. You'll thank me later." Argus said smugly and leaned once again on the lamp post.

Samson left Argus with a nervous feeling in his stomach. He didn't much like the sound of Argus's surprise.

The second surprising thing that week happened as soon as Samson got back to the house. He noticed a strange car in the driveway. It was a Ford Focus with a couple of Air Force bumper stickers on the back. One said "Aim High." Samson always liked that one.

He walked inside to find his mother chatting with a small and thin balding man in white shirt sleeves with a thin navy tie and nicely pressed navy pants. He had a neatly trimmed mustache that levitated above his upper lip.

"Oh, there he is. Samson come here. There's someone I think you will like to meet." Mom said as the visitor rose and turned to face Samson.

"Captain Mark McKain," he said extending his hand to greet Samson. He had a very nasally voice. It was a bit grating and made it hard for Samson to concentrate. "It's a pleasure to finally meet you Samson." Samson reluctantly gave Captain McKain his hand and glanced over to his mother with a 'who is this guy?' look. Captain McKain took Samson's hand in a deliberately firm handshake and gave him a forced smile.

"Sorry it took so long to get in touch with you, but it took a while to go over all of the data for the region. I'm head of the New England branch of the AOPA, so I have several states to look after." Captain McKain said with pride. He was clearly a bit of a nerd. Samson was sure he spent much of his time going over data. He blinked and looked at the captain with a blank stare. He had no idea what this guy was talking about.

Mom finally spoke up to help him out. "Captain McKain is a pilot. Apparently, they were very impressed with your testing at the flying camp in Danbury."

Samson still didn't know what this was about, but nodded his head regardless. "OK." he said drawing out the K.

"Yes, you showed great aptitude for flying. In fact, you were the highest ranked student in the whole region in the 12-16 year old age group. It's extremely unusual for a twelve year old to score so high, and someone who was a first time camp attendee. We are always on the lookout for young people with your potential." Captain McKain continued. "I've come by to see if you would be interested in taking a more intensive course. It is a course we only recruit the best and brightest. Many of our students become the best jet fighter pilots in the Air Force."

Samson was dumbfounded. He couldn't speak. He looked to his Mother and she smiled at him.

"Is this for real?" he asked his mother at last.

"As far as I can tell. It seems legit." Mom answered.

"I can assure you, we do not make this offer to just anyone. You will actually be the only twelve year old in the class and one of only three twelve year olds to ever be invited in the history of the program." Captain McKain confessed.

"I'll be thirteen in a month." Samson stated absentmindedly since he still didn't know what to say.

"We better get started then," Captain McKain said with a smirk - he was trying to be charming but it was coming off a bit creepy. Samson still couldn't get past the mustache. It looked like a fuzzy caterpillar hanging above his lip. It came alive when he spoke. It was mesmerizing.

"So what will we do?" Samson asked, still staring at the mustache.

"We will teach you how to fly, of course," Capt McKain began. "The first thing we do is help you get your pilot's license. Then we test your aptitude to determine what type of airplane you might best pilot, from the largest planes like the new Boeing Dreamliner 787, to a fighter jet like the F-22 Raptor."

"Seriously?" Samson asked still dubious about the whole situation. This was almost as cool as spontaneously combusting.

"Seriously." Captain McKain said, still smiling at Samson. He could see the gears turning in Samson's head. He had seen this same scene in many other households.

Samson turned to his mother. "If this is for real, then I REALLY want to do it." He looked at his mother with the first hint of true desire in his face. His mother's face, however, went from a pleasant smile to one of concern. This couldn't be good.

"Captain McKain," Mom addressed the visitor, " this is an incredible offer, but I hate to even think about how much this would cost. The short four day camp we had him in was almost beyond our means. I don't think we will be able to afford it," she said, turning to Samson, who looked crestfallen. "But, I guess it doesn't hurt to look into it."

"The best part about this offer, Mrs. Presley," Captain McKain said, the caterpillar above his lip leapt up towards his nostrils, "is that the course is completely free. All of the expenses are taken care of. Samson would get one-on-one instruction and be involved in some great group lectures. We do, in fact, have an opening for orientation this week if the young gentleman is available."

"Really?" Samson said ecstatic. This was beyond belief. Well, beyond normal belief, not including the incredible events of the summer so far. "This is the best summer ever!" He jumped up and gave his mother a hug.

"Ok, ok, Samson. Calm down. We need to find out a little more about the program and make sure this is a good thing for you," his mother said rationally.

"Are you kidding? It sounds awesome!" Samson continued to jump around.

"Captain Mckain, I'm sure you have some information you can leave for me and my husband to review. When would you need an answer?" Mom inquired.

"The orientation is on Friday, so if you let me know by tomorrow, I should still be able to get him in," Captain Mckain answered. Samson began running about the room with his arms out like an airplane making jet engine noises. "I think he's rather excited now," he observed and stood to leave.

"You bet I am," Samson said, and ran over and joyfully shook the captain's hand. "Thank you so much, I'm sure I'll see you on Friday. If I don't, I'll probably come anyway because I'll be needing new parents." At this Samson flew off up the stairs.

"It sounds like a wonderful opportunity," Mom said showing Captain McKain to the door, "but I need to talk to my husband. I'm sure you understand."

"I would be worried if you didn't take some time to think about it, Mrs. Presley. Flying is a serious profession that shouldn't be taken lightly. We do our best to not only teach flying but discipline, respect and pride. It does take these things to make a good pilot." Captain McKain clicked his heels, nodded to Mom, and headed out the door. It was then that Mom noticed he had a slight limp. She wondered if it was an injury he received in combat as she closed the door and turned her attention to the pamphlet he left.

The house was abuzz with excitement by the time Dad got home. Samson had set up an passenger airplane in they yard with cardboard boxes and miscellaneous yard chairs. Thisbe was the flight attendant and was serving lemonade to the passengers, Wylde and Castilia. As it turned out, Wylde was not a passenger but the first mate and Castilia was the rich rock star celebrity who owned the private jet which was now headed to LA, so she could receive a Grammy for best new artist. Mom and Dad sat on the terrace reading the material and discussing the school while watching their children engrossed in make believe.

After an internet search and a few phone calls, Mom and Dad felt comfortable this was legitimate and called Captain McKain to let him know Samson would be attending the orientation on Friday. Everyone cheered. They couldn't wait for Samson to take them up in an airplane.

CHAPTER 25

Flight School

Samson found that the next few days flew by, no pun intended. He spent most of his time on the computer airplane simulation games he loved to play. He wanted to make sure he had a leg up before he even started. His mother tried to tell him that playing video games was no way to learn to fly, but Samson insisted it was giving him the skills he needed to fly on the very first day.

Friday morning came and Samson was up with the rising sun. He was so excited he had a hard time eating breakfast. He was expected at orientation by nine AM and he made his mother walk out the door at 8 o'clock for the thirty minute ride to the airport. He was the first student to arrive and found Captain Mckain inside the terminal building straightening up the room that was to be used as the classroom.

"I do like punctuality, Samson Presley. It is a sign of responsibility and respect." Captain McKain said as Samson walked into the room. "It is good to see you. I was very happy to receive your parent's call the other day. Please find a seat, I still have a few things to take care of." He continued to busy himself in his preparations as Samson took a seat at the front of the room.

The Danbury airport is a small local airport that services four to six seat single propeller airplanes. There was an occasional private jet, of course, but most of the traffic was local private owners of Cessnas or Piper single engine aircraft. The airport had just one north south and one east west runway, as well as a small control tower.

All the other students began filing in around 8:50 and they all looked to be in high school as far as Samson could tell. He felt very young and small. Captain McKain got started precisely at 9 AM. He began by taking attendance. Everyone was present.

"Welcome, everyone. I'm Captain McKain and I will be your instructor for this course and many others. You will learn to fly. First, however, you must learn about the machine that will carry us. We need to know how it works, how it is put together, what we can do with it, and how to fix it. So let's get started, shall we?"

Samson listened as the Captain began to explain the fundamentals of flying. The amount of information he covered was astounding. He was talking about pistons, fuel pumps, ball bearings and fetzer valves. Samson's head was spinning after the first ten minutes. Being the smallest and youngest student, Samson was very self concious. He had so many questions he didn't know where to begin, but he didn't want to sound stupid in front of the other students so he just kept his mouth shut. After a few more minutes, he was completely lost and began to panic. He looked over at the other students who all seemed to be calmly taking notes and understanding every word Captain McKain was uttering. Samson was sweating. This was a disaster.

His flying career was over before it ever began. He should have spent more time flying the single engine plane on the video simulator, he thought. He was too busy flying the big commercial 747s. Blast!

Samson couldn't concentrate for the rest of the class. By the end he was utterly depressed. 'Epic Fail' was all that continued to course through his jumbled mind. The class ended at exactly 10 o'clock. Captain Mckain handed some papers out to the class. Samson had no idea what they were. He lowered his head and slowly retreated out of the door to find his mother waiting for him just outside. He walked around the car and slumped heavily into the passenger seat.

"So, how was it?" his mother asked brightly as she pulled away from the curb and headed home.

Samson was crushed. His hopes and dreams of becoming a pilot had been destroyed in one short hour. He hadn't even made it through one class. He was pathetic. All of his excitement and emotion from the last few days turned into a heavy burden of frustration and disappointment. Samson tried to control it but it was too much and now bubbled to the surface. He could feel it exploding like a volcano. He started bawling hysterically, his head buried in his hands.

"Good gracious, what's the matter?" Mom asked, surprised, but with that soothing motherly tone. "Are you OK?"

Samson tried to compose himself but he had never in his life been so disappointed. How could he let something he wanted so badly slip right through his fingers. He continued to cry, letting the disappointment wash over him. After a few minutes he could feel the tension begin to subside and was able to look up. He saw his mother looking at him with concern in her eyes and lightly rubbing his shoulders. She had pulled off the road.

"What's the matter, honey?" she said.

"I'm too stupid, Mom. I didn't understand any of it." Samson said sniffling. "Not a single word. It was ridiculous. There's no way I can be a pilot. It's over."

"Giving up that quickly?" Mom said still in the soothing Mom voice."It doesn't even seem like you gave it a fair try."

"But I didn't even understand enough to even try!" Samson's voice rose in frustration.

"Why don't you clear your head and calm yourself. Just sit back and relax and we'll figure this out when we get home." Mom suggested.

Samson nodded, then laid his head back and closed his watery eyes as Mom accelerated back onto the road.

"Mom." Samson said after a while

"Yes dear." She answered.

"Can we not tell everyone what happened when we get home?" He asked hopefully.

"Of course. Why don't we stop at the diner for a snack and talk it over." She suggested.

He nodded and sniffled again.

When they stopped at the diner, Samson realized he was famished. He didn't eat any breakfast because he was too excited. Now the food was much-needed comfort. As they ate, Mom was able to convince him to look at the study material and concentrate more on the material and less on the video simulations.

"No one said this would be easy. If this is something that you really want, then you should put forth the effort that is required to achieve it," she said.

As alway, Mom had sage words of advice. After eating, Samson felt much better and was able to organize his mind. On the way home, he looked at the handouts and some of the information did seem familiar. Perhaps he did pick up something while Captain Mckain was speaking. He decided he would spend the next week trying to bring himself up to speed.

When they got home he went straight to his room to review the sheets and see if he could figure out where the gaps were. He resolved to even ask Castilia to help him - but only if he got desperate.

CHAPTER 26

The Epic Sleepover

Studying went well the next few days. Castilia helped Samson get organized. He had not realized that he really didn't know how to study. He never gave it much thought, and had only ever put in just enough effort to get by. That certainly never involved being neat and organized. Castilia showed him how to break the information down and start a notebook of notes and relevant information. Wylde was very helpful in finding great websites that were full of additional information. After two days of hard work, Samson felt much better and had a renewed vigor and confidence.

By Tuesday, Samson was in good shape. He could tell you the major parts of a single propeller engine and knew how they went together. He could also describe how a simple combustion engine worked.

Mom reminded him that he was going over to a sleepover at Argus's house the next day which Samson had completely forgotten about. He didn't much care about Argus's epic adventure. It was going to take him away from his current focus.

Mom made it clear that he could not back out now and said a sleepover would be a nice break for him.

Samson continued with his studies until Wednesday afternoon when Mom took him over to Argus's house.

"I've got everything all set. It's going to be awesome!" Argus declared when Samson walked into his room. Argus and Professor Finch lived in a small two story white Victorian farmhouse with a small front porch and single story addition to the rear which just so happened to allow Argus to easily and quietly escape from his bedroom window and climb down a ladder he had propped up against the house for just such an occasion.

Argus was just as excited as Samson had been about the flying course. Upon his arrival, Argus immediately pulled Samson outside so he could fill him in on the plans as Mom spent a few minutes chatting with Professor Finch.

"Samson!" Mom yelled as she saw the two of them running toward the door. "Where are your manners? Acknowledge your host."

"Hello, Professor Finch." Samson said and returned with an outstretched hand to greet Argus's father.

"Hello, young man." Professor Finch said smiling. "Welcome to our modest domicile. Please make yourself at home and don't hesitate to ask for anything you may need."

"Right. Let's go." Argus said pulling Samson along.

"Thank you." Samson managed to reply to Professor Finch, and then he was thrown out of the door.

"OK, so we are going to meet up with Jimmy Mcmillan and Tyler Brooks just after midnight down the street." Argus began once they got clear of the house.

"Great." Samson thought sarcastically. This was already sounding like a bad idea. Jimmy and Tyler were generally known to be hoodlums in Westville. The two of them had been involved in almost every underhanded scheme Samson could think of. They were most notorious for painting "Can't" and "Jimty" on several stop signs in the area. It was obvious to everyone they did it but the police didn't have any other evidence other than one anonymous tip and the name "Jimty" that was painted on the signs. Jimmy and Tyler both flatly denied any wrong doing. It was rumored that Howard Mitchell was the anonymous tipper.

Howard was a nerdy brainiac who was a hall monitor and had a serious relationship with justice. He'd report anyone for the slightest infraction. He was always right and never gave anyone a break. This did not help his popularity. He was an equal opportunity snitch who did not stray from the rules. He roamed the halls and heard everything. No one likes a rat, especially in sixth grade. Snitches get stitches. At any rate, the anonymous tipper did not come forward as a witness, so Jimmy and Tyler were never charged for lack of evidence.

"It's going to be epic." Argus continued.

Samson kept quiet. He figured the less he knew the better - plausible deniability was his only hope. But every second they got closer to midnight, the more Samson was dreading it. In retrospect, Samson thought this would have been a good time to fake an illness, or even chip a tooth or something, but unfortunately his boyish stupidity kept him following along. Perhaps, however, it was destiny because it did turn out to be a good thing he was there.

Much to his disappointment, Mom was gone by the time they got back inside. Samson had lost his window of escape. It was just a waiting game now. Argus was acting weird, but it was just because he was overly excited.

"Look," Samson said after a while of wandering around doing nothing, "we need to do something to occupy ourselves for a while. It's a long time to midnight."

"You are absolutely right. It's time I showed you something." Argus said with a grin on his face. "I think I can trust you with this...and if I can't, I'll just have to kill you."

Samson wasn't sure if he was kidding or not. In fact, he was always unsure if Argus was kidding but followed him outside again.

"Dad, we'll be outside for a while." Argus yelled as they were leaving.

"Certainly, but be back in about an hour, I'll have the burgers on the grill." Professor Finch yelled back from somewhere inside the house.

Argus lead Samson to the backyard and then into the woods and past the fence that bordered the lawn.

"This is the Nature Conservancy area; no one can build a house back here. There are no trails, except for this one that I made." Argus said as they started into the woods.

"Cool. Do you ever see any bears?" Samson asked.

"No, never seen a bear, but I'm pretty sure I saw a bobcat once. I've got a little hideout back here that allows me to check things out without being seen. No one knows about this so if you tell anyone I will seriously break your neck." Argus said, leading them down a steep hill to a small brook which they crossed by jumping from stone to stone.

Not too much further Argus abruptly stopped and announced, "We're here."

Samson looked about and saw a bunch of scrub brush that descended down the next hill. "We're where?" Samson said still looking for a campsite or something.

"Haha. Isn't it great!" Argus said smiling. He moved toward a clump of bushes and reached down to grab something. Much to Samson's surprise he pulled open a secret hatch. It was a small rectangular opening just large enough for Argus to get down. He promptly turned around and lowered himself down into the hole on what Samson assumed was some sort of ladder. Argus disappeared. "OK I made it. You can come down now. Close the hatch on your way."

Samson paused for a moment. This was really weird. Did Argus have a Chamber of Transition too? Samson nervously peered down the hole and found it wasn't dark at all nor was it very deep. He swung himself around and descended the ladder, closing the top hatch as he was instructed. He found himself in a small, partially underground room that seemed to be very well constructed. The back wall and the floor were earth that had been dug out. The opposite wall was built of wood and had a series of small openings, all of which had small shutters that hinged at the top. Argus was in the process of opening the shutters to lighten the room and tie them to the ceiling. The ceiling was supported by wood beams, and corrugated sheet metal covered the whole area. There was a small table with what looked like a chemistry set on it. A single chair was beside the table and a series of old blankets lay across what looked to be a fairly comfortable bed.

"Wow," was all Samson could say.

"Yeah, I know, right? When you don't have any friends, you have a lot of free time. My dad is not around a lot either so I spend a lot of time here." Argus said looking around with pride.

"You built all this, yourself?" Samson asked flabbergasted. "This is awesome!"

"I can sit here quietly and watch rabbits, foxes, raccoons, deer, whatever, walk right up to the windows. They don't even know I'm here. Mostly, I come down here and read. Sometimes I do chemistry experiments, like the one I've been doing lately. Let me show you," Argus said motioning to the table.

"You read?" Samson said before he could stop himself.

"Of course I read, numbnuts," Argus said rolling his eyes and punching Samson in the shoulder for good measure. "I love to read. Just not in school. They want you to read the most boring stuff ever."

Samson couldn't argue with that. They did make you read the most boring stuff ever.

"So I got this recipe for a stink bomb off the internet. Matches and some ammonia and I put it in these eggs for easy carrying and distribution. We'll make good use of these tonight," Argus said holding one up for inspection.

"How did you get it into the eggs?" Samson asked.

"That, my friend, is a good question, but I'm not ready to give up all my secrets just yet," Argus answered with a look of satisfaction on his face.

The boys spent the time before dinner happily in Argus's hideout. Samson was amazed that Argus built this all by himself. The boy was quite skilled and continued to surprise. They headed back to the house, ate dinner, watched a movie, then went to bed. Samson had forgotten about the night's planned misadventure and dozed off.

"Dude, it's time to go. My Dad's snoring up a storm." Argus said in a whisper, shaking Samson awake.

"Wha? Huh?" Samson replied in a daze.

"Get up, Doofus!" Argus said, no longer whispering, and pulled him out of the bed. Samson fell to the floor with a thunk. "Quiet! You'll wake my Dad." Argus said, whispering again and looking around cautiously.

Samson got dressed and followed Argus, tiptoeing out of the house. Once they made it to the front yard Argus took off running, which startled Samson out of his malaise, and he quickly followed.

Up on the next corner, Samson could see two dark figures standing under the streetlight. He began to get very nervous - the figures seemed to be staring at them as they approached and they were not moving. Then he noticed the bikes.

"Samson," Argus said quietly, trying to catch his breath. "You know Jimmy and Tyler."

"Yeah. Hi guys." Samson said as he approached. Jimmy and Tyler both nodded, looking Samson up and down in disapproval. Neither boy said anything.

"I see you brought the gear and the bikes...Is everything here?" Argus said. Jimmy and Tyler nodded again as Argus checked the contents and was apparently satisfied.

Argus went over to the bushes and pulled out a nice black mountain bike with a huge shock absorber on the front fork. He gave that to Samson to hold as he reached back into the bushes. This time he pulled out a small pink bike with a white banana seat and pink and white streamers coming out of the handle bars.

"What the hell is this?" Argus asked Jimmy.

"I dunno. My other bike had a flat tire so I had to borrow my little sister's." Jimmy answered with a snicker.

"You moron. How is Samson supposed to keep up with us on this?" Argus was angry, but amused. Jimmy started laughing and Argus gave him a hard look "If you mess this up for me tonight, there will be hell to pay." Jimmy stopped laughing.

"Really, it's the only bike I had." Jimmy pleaded.

"It's OK, I don't care. It's not a big deal." Samson jumped in. The sooner this was over the better.

They all donned a backpack and took off on the bikes. It was hard for Samson to keep up, but he did his best. The other three boys were not the most fit so after the first few minutes, it became much easier. They wound around Westville, taking dirt shortcuts through backyards and parks. They rode for about 10 minutes until Argus finally stopped at an unassuming suburban ranch house somewhere in the middle of Westville.

"This is it." Argus said, dismounting his bike and hurrying over to a clump of trees. The other boys followed suit. "Give me your backpacks," Argus ordered.

"What's that?" Samson said staring into the darkness. He thought he saw something move in the shadows toward the back of the house. They were all a bit on edge. They stood there quietly staring into the darkness, listening to the silence.

"Dude, don't do that." Argus said, and began unpacking. Samson realized what they were about to do and had a funny feeling in his stomach. There was a wide array of toilet paper, eggs, whipped cream and something in a large container.

"What's that?" Samson asked getting worried.

"That's gasoline. We're going to spell out "DWEEB" in the lawn with the gas. The gas will kill the grass and you'll be able to read it for ages." Argus explained, barely containing his glee.

"Argus," Samson began slowly. "Whose house is this?"

"Howard Mitchell." Argus answered mischievously with a big smile on his face.

Samson looked at the boys and saw the excitement in their faces. It was revenge time for them and they couldn't wait. He would be party to it too. "No, I can't do this. This isn't right." Samson said in disgust.

"See! I told you he would wuss out," Tyler announced too loudly.

"Dude, don't be a spoilsport." Argus chided. "You have to admit, this kid deserves anything we dish out."

"No Argus, no one deserves to be publicly humiliated and have their house destroyed." Samson said more sternly.

"Nothing we are doing is permanent. It will all go away in a couple of weeks. I made sure of that. It's not like we are giving him a good beating, although that would be more fun and more what he deserves." Argus argued.

"This is stupid and I'm not doing it," Samson said and got on the girl bike.

"You can't take my sister's bike, loser." Jimmy said standing up.

Samson looked Jimmy up and down. He could probably beat him in a fair fight, but Jimmy didn't fight fair and Tyler would certainly join in too. "Fine! Take the stupid bike. I can run back home faster anyway." Samson said turning away and began walking down the street.

"Samson, come on, we aren't hurting anyone." Argus pleaded one last time.

"Let him go. He'd just ruin it anyway." Tyler said as he took the gas and started pouring out letters in the lawn. Samson looked back one last time. "How do you spell dweeb?" He heard Tyler ask as he walked on in the darkness.

CHAPTER 27

The Choice

Samson was furious. He was furious at himself for getting into this situation. He was furious that he didn't stop them. He was furious that he was walking away. The dark still air was infused with the sounds of the night which helped calm him. He remembered that Mrs. Goodwyn said he'd have to make a choice and maybe this was that moment. He decided he had to do something. He turned around and started running back toward the house that was being defaced determined to stop Argus and the boys. He was just a couple of houses away when something made him stop. He looked down to his chest to see his medallion glowing red hot. That was when all hell broke loose.

In an instant, a bright flash of light and a deafening explosion threw Samson to the ground. He opened his eyes to see a giant fireball mushrooming up in the sky. It illuminated the area like sunlight.

"Oh my God!" Samson said out loud as he got up and raced to the house. Everything was on fire. Argus, Jimmy and Tyler were laying on the ground in the front yard unconscious, bits of burning house were scattered all around them. Argus was bleeding from his head and Tyler's arm was laying in an unnatural way. Samson grabbed each one in turn and pulled them to safety in the next yard. When he finally managed to get Argus to a safe distance, he thought he heard a baby crying coming from the house. The reality of what had happened didn't hit him until that moment. Howard and his family were probably still in the house. He didn't hesitate to think any longer but raced headlong toward the front door. The garage was completely missing and the front of house was fully engulfed in flames now. As Samson got closer, the heat didn't seem to bother him so he kept moving forward. The front door was hanging off the hinges and open now. Samson was able to jump through the burning opening into the house. Flames were climbing all of the walls in the entry hall, but Samson could see the rest of the house seemed to be unaffected at the moment. Smoke was billowing everywhere, but he saw a hallway to the left and ran down it. The screaming grew louder as he was coming down the hall. He turned into a bedroom to his right that looked like a nursery and found Howard's two year old sister wailing at the top of her lungs, standing at the side of her crib. He jerked her out of the crib and ran back out of the hall and then to the back of the house. The glass door to the back yard had shattered in the blast and Samson jumped through it with the baby and ran to a play house at the rear of the property where he sat the little girl down and told her to stay. She sat there crying and watched him run back into the house.

Once back in the house, he ran back in the direction he come. Samson noticed more doors in the hall and found what looked like Howard's room which had started to burn. Howard was nowhere to be seen. The next room was the master bedroom and Mrs. Mitchell was laying face down on the floor next to her bed unconscious. He curiously noticed an empty vodka bottle laying near her head. He shook her and she moved and said something indiscernible.

"Mrs. Mitchell, you have to get up!" Samson yelled with urgency. She slowly rolled over and let out a tired sigh. The bitter smell of alcohol stung his nostrils and Samson winced. She was definitely sloshed. With serious effort, Samson was able to help Mrs. Mitchell off the floor and put her arm around his shoulder and begin to drag her out of the house. Luckily she was not a big woman. He took her to the playhouse and laid her carefully down in front of the door where the little girl was still sitting and crying. Once again Samson raced back into the burning home. This time the smoke was incredibly thick. It was burning his eyes. He began calling "Howard! Howard!" This time he turned right and found the family room which was in complete disarray. the furniture was all upside down and thrown into the corner. The large TV on the wall was cracked and reflected the flames now moving rapidly into the room. As he was about to leave to look elsewhere he noticed a tiny hand under the overturned sofa. He found Howard under the furniture and pulled him free without much trouble. Howard was very small for a sixth grader. Samson hoisted him over his shoulder and ran back outside and placed him beside his mother.

Once more Samson headed back into the house. He went back into the foyer so he could head down the hall again to see if he could find Mr. Mitchell. This time, however, he didn't make it any further. The room seemed to inhale a breath of air then another explosion rocked the house and threw Samson out of the front door. He landed hard in the yard rolling on the grass. He stood up and looked back at the house, it was now completely in flames. He looked down at himself and found his shirt was on fire as well. This surprised him more than anything as he was not burned by the flames, but his reaction was the same as it would have been regardless. He quickly ripped off the shirt and threw it burning to the ground. He stared at his shirt in disbelief. "What the hell just happened?" he thought, as he heard sirens approaching in the distance. He turned toward the road and saw neighbors gathering on the street, looking at him with their mouths gaping. Some others were looking over Argus, Jimmy, and Tyler.

Firemen and police suddenly swarmed the area. Samson had moved off to the side and began slowly working his way away from the confusion. The Firemen uncoiled their hoses and began fighting the flames. Men were shouting orders and running everywhere. Paramedics were attending to the boys and police were busy asking the bystanders questions. Samson was still scanning the scene when he noticed one of the neighbors talking to the police and pointing in his direction.

Samson panicked. He wasn't supposed to be there. He lived no where near here. How was he going to explain this. His Mom and Dad were going to kill him. He slowly turned and began to walk away.

"Hey! You! Boy!" Samson heard the voices trying to get his attention. His panic got the better of him and he started running.

"Stop!"

That was the last thing he was going to do. He was terrified and just wanted to get out of there. He ran as fast as he could, though bushes and brambles, around trees and over fences. All he could hear was the fast drumming of his heart and his straining breath. He looked back to see if he was being followed but was immediately hit from the side by something very large. It knocked the breath out of him and he landed hard face down on the ground. He felt a knee in his back as someone was grabbing his wrists and forcing them behind his back.

"Now why did you have to go and do that for?" said a woman's voice breathlessly as he was jerked up to his feet. The policewoman was breathing hard but not as hard as Samson. She spun him around and looked at him annoyed.

"I just had this uniform cleaned and now look at it." she said, leading him back toward the glowing light in the distance. "Shoot, I think that's a grass stain."

"How did you catch me?" Samson finally said once he was able to breath again.

"Honey, a lot of men much faster and older than you have asked that same question." She said grinning. "The more important question was why did you run?"

"I was scared. I'm not supposed to be here." Samson said looking down at the ground.

"Well, that much is clear, sugar. Unfortunately, we'll need to straighten this all out down at the station." She answered as she led Samson to one of the police cars on the street with its red and blue lights twirling silently. She opened the door and put her hand on his head to help him into the back seat. Samson awkwardly fell into the seat and she slammed the door shut.

"The station!? The Station? I'm being arrested?" Samson thought. "Crap. My life is over." He was too worried and scared to cry. This was all too surreal. He desperately wanted his Mom and Dad even though he knew this was going to kill them. Samson didn't look out the window, he didn't move, he just held his head down and tried to breathe.

Suddenly the car door opened and another police officer poked his head in.

"Son, I'm Sargent O'Malley - this EMT is going to check you out to make sure you are not hurt. Is that OK?

"Sure, I guess," Samson said still in a daze.

"What's your name, son?"

"Samson."

"Samson, I'm going to help you get out of the car so I can check you out, OK?" a soothing female voice asked.

"OK." Samson said as hands pulled him gently out of the car.

"How old are you?

"Twelve," he answered.

"He's only twelve." The EMT said to the police officer as she continued to look him over. "Does anything hurt? Are you hurt?"

"No." he said quietly still looking at the ground.

"He seems to be fine. He's dirty, but that's about it. I can see his pants are burned and singed in places but his skin doesn't show any sign of blistering or redness. He's very lucky."

"Who are your parents, Samson?" Sargent O'Malley asked.

Samson looked up at him scared. As much as he wanted his mom to give him hug and tell him everything will be all right, he wouldn't be able to bear their disappointment. "We can't tell my parents. This will kill them. Please don't tell my parents," he pleaded.

"Son, we have to notify your parents. We don't have a choice, and neither do you." the Sargent replied.

Samson stopped talking at that point. His mind was racing. It seemed like people were asking him more questions, but he didn't hear them and didn't respond. Someone led him back to the car and helped him into the backseat again. The door closed.

After what seemed like an eternity, the fast policewoman got into the driver's seat and started up the engine. "You OK back there, honey?" she said as she accelerated down the street.

"Yes," Samson said softly. "I guess."

"What's your name, sugar?

"Samson."

"Samson, do your parents know where you are?"

"No, they don't."

"Would you like for me to call them?"

"No!" Samson started to panic again. "You can't call them - they think I'm at a sleep over."

"I think the jig is up on that one, honey. It's probably best if we call them. Don't you think?"

"Please don't call them." Samson begged.

"Honey, they will want to know that you are OK, no matter where you are."

Samson thought about this and reluctantly gave the officer the information. She quickly radioed this in. They arrived at the police station soon thereafter and he was taken to a small room with a table and a chair. The handcuffs were removed and they gave him a shirt and some water and left him with the fast police officer.

"Do you want to know how I caught you?" she asked after a moment.

Samson looked up. "Sure," he said but he really didn't care.

"I was third in the nation in college in the 400 meters. That wasn't too long ago. There's still not too many people I can't catch. It really wasn't a fair race." she said smiling.

Samson managed a half-hearted smile back.

"So do you want to tell me what happened back there?" she asked, still smiling.

Samson looked at her and decided she might actually listen to him. He started with the invitation to sleep over at Argus's house and recounted the entire story. She sat in front of him listening quietly and nodding at times. She stopped him a couple of times to ask a quick question. "So he had gas but no matches?" and "Did you see any other fireworks or explosives in the backpacks?"

When Samson got to the part about helping the Mitchells outside he remembered something.

"Oh my gosh! I never found Mr. Mitchell. Is he OK?" he asked.

"He was out of town," she assured him. "He wasn't in the house. Everyone got out."

Samson finish up his story and felt much better.

"So you just happened to be there when the house exploded? Is that what you are saying?" the officer asked when Samson was done.

"Yes." Samson answered getting a little worried.

"But you weren't at the house when it exploded?"

"That's right."

"Are you saying your friends caused the explosion?"

"Ummm. No. Wait. I have no idea. I wasn't there." Samson explained again.

"Uh huh. Then you single handedly pulled everyone away and out of the burning house without getting burned and hurt yourself. Is that correct?"

"Yes." He could see where this was going.

"That sounds a little far fetched don't you think?" she asked.

"I don't know. It's the truth." Samson said deflated.

"The Truth." She said and nodded at him. She stood up and walked to the door. "I'll be back in a minute. Do you need anything?"

Samson shook his head and she left. Exhaustion set in. He realized he must have been up all night at this point. All he wanted to do was to go to sleep.

A short while later the door opened again. Sargent O'Malley stepped in.

"Son, I have to tell you...this doesn't look good," He said plopping a large folder on the table in front of him. "Your father is here filling out paper work for your release into his custody and he's given us permission to ask you a few more questions."

Samson looked at the Sargent with bloodshot eyes but did not answer. He was now terrified.

"What kind of explosive did you use on the house?" the Sargent asked calmly.

This got Samson's attention. "What?" he said in a shocked voice.

"The neighbors said you ran out of the house just before the last explosion. So what did you use?" the Sargent continued.

"What?! Are you kidding? I didn't run out, I was blown out!" Samson yelled exasperated.

"How do you explain the fact that you have no burns, cuts or bruises on your body? In fact, you are the only one involved that is completely unharmed."

Samson thought of the medallion and his power and decided if he told them the truth they'd really think he was crazy. "I don't know." He finally said deflated.

"You don't know." O'Malley paused here and shook his head. "Son, you are in serious trouble here. We are looking at arson and six counts of attempted murder. Lucky for you everyone made it out with minor burns and some lacerations. Two of the boys are in the hospital being treated. Do you understand how serious this is?" O'Malley stared at Samson.

"I didn't do anything." Samson said quietly and looked down at his shoes trying to process what he'd been told.

At that moment, the door opened and his father walked in. Dad hurried over and gave his son a huge hug and whispered, "Are you OK?" in his ear. Samson exploded into tears and wept as his emotions finally flooded out. They stayed like that for a while until Samson was able to compose himself. Samson finally looked up at his father who looked miserable. He looked old and tired. The bags under his eyes made him look desperate and depressed. His eyes were red and swollen, and it was clear he'd been crying. Samson never thought he could feel worse than he had, but the sight of his father's overwhelming disappointment took him to a place he'd never been before - sheer and utter misery.

"Let's go," Dad said with a sad smile.

They rose and started to the door.

"We'll need to see him tomorrow after he's rested," Sargent O'Malley said as they left.

Dad nodded to him and led Samson out the door.

The ride home was long and quiet. Samson didn't know what to say. Apparently, his father, for once, didn't either. They arrived home as the rising sun caused the sky to turn from black to a deep ominous blue. Low clouds in the east were glowing orange at the horizon like fire.

Samson followed his father inside the house and saw his mother at the kitchen table staring silently into the darkness. Mom looked desperately tired as she slumped over a cold cup of coffee. She slowly turned her head toward her son as they approached. Samson looked into his mother's bloodshot eyes and saw a misery he'd never seen before. He stopped at the doorway and wanted to plead his case but his mother turned her head away from him in disgust and put up her hand for him to stop. Samson slowly turned and headed upstairs to his bedroom, his heart broken by the injustice of it all. He climbed into his bed with his clothes on and quickly fell into a fitful sleep.

CHAPTER 28

Birthday

Samson slept for the entire day and woke early the next morning still not able to believe his predicament. The next few days were nightmarish with trips back and forth to the police station where he was asked the same questions time and again. No one believed his story. They couldn't get past the fact that he had not been harmed and that was proof of his guilt. Mom and Dad, in fact, succumbed to the same conclusion. His only solace was his brother and sisters who knew his secret and therefore his story made perfect sense. He went over it with them in detail and the confession made him stronger. At least someone was on his side but they really couldn't do anything for him.

The police finally tired of asking Samson questions and requested that he come back the following Wednesday once they had time to interview the Mitchells. Argus and Tyler were still in the hospital. Argus took the brunt of the explosion and had been unconscious for a couple of days. The police were waiting for him recover enough to question him. Tyler had a broken arm and some cuts and bruises, but wasn't talking as was his modus operandi. Jimmy was released the night of the explosion and his parents had taken him to Vermont for the weekend. He was glad to learn that the Mitchells were all fine. Howard had some cuts and a few second degree burns but would make a full recovery.

Mom and Dad were being as supportive as they could. They listened to Samson's story and said the right things, but Samson could tell they didn't believe him. Mom was always upset and said she loved him but he could see the heartbreak in her bloodshot and tired eyes. This breach of conduct and trust had destroyed her. This was the hardest part for Samson. He was ready and willing to accept responsibility for his actions but he couldn't bear the affect he was having on his mother.

Next to his mother's disappointment, the worst thing of all was the realization on Sunday that he had missed flight school. All his hard work was for nothing. It was another devastating blow. It was just another dream dashed by the insane events the other night. Samson wondered if things could get any worse, and, of course they did.

Samson had completely forgotten his thirteenth birthday was on Monday. It was supposed to be a wonderful milestone, the day he became a teenager. It didn't really matter much - it was the last nail in his already finished coffin. There would be no birthday party or cake or presents. He was in so much trouble he didn't feel like celebrating anything. His parents had him on lockdown and wouldn't let him out of the house. It wasn't like he wanted to go anywhere or do anything anyway.

Castillia, Thisbe and Wylde wanted to, at the very least, get Samson out of the house on Monday to enjoy the sunshine and try and forget about the issue at hand for the afternoon. After a sad lunch of peanut butter sandwiches (Mom hadn't cooked since Samson was arrested), they were able to get Mom and Dad to agree to let him out of the house for a while.

They decided to have a nice picnic birthday dinner for Samson. Thisbe went wild making a very elaborate meal with all of Samson's favorites. Well, actually, Samson's favorites were pizza and hamburgers and she didn't know how to make pizza and they didn't have any hamburger meat. But he did love bagels and smoked salmon, so she made him that. She fixed a garden salad with ranch dressing, another of his favorites, and some mixed fruit. Castilia helped her bake a cake, which made a formidable mess in the kitchen which took them half of the morning clean up. Wylde pitched in and scrubbed the pots and pans. For a bunch of pre-teens, it was a magnificent spread. Thisbe packed the blanket and some sparkling lemonade and even had some candles for the cake. They only had chocolate icing but made an "S" out of strawberries in the middle.

They were all set for the picnic by two o'clock and they dragged the birthday boy out of his room and up to the knoll. They set up the blanket under the old oak tree. It was a nice late summer day. It wasn't too hot, and clouds blanketed the sky. The wind was mildly blowing and gave a little relief to the humidity, but there was darkness on the horizon. It looked like a storm could be rolling in for the evening. For now, though, the sun was still peeking out from behind the clouds and Thisbe set everything up under the canopy of the oak tree.

They sat and ate under the tree and enjoyed the breeze and the proximity of each other's company. No one had to say a word for Samson to understand the love and support he was receiving now. The fog that had surrounded him for days now lifted and he felt normal again.

"Thanks guys," he said at last. "I really needed this."

"Happy Birthday, big brother," Wylde answered, and threw him an irregularly shaped present roughly wrapped in newspaper. Samson opened it to find a crudely carved wooden bird. He could tell Wylde worked hours on this. It was beautiful. He held it up for everyone to see.

"It's amazing Wylde. Thanks." Samson said appreciatively.

"It's a Phoenix." Wylde explained. "It rises from the ashes once it is burned down."

Samson nodded in acknowledgment of Wylde's intent.

Thisbe handed him a roll of paper tied with a large blue bow and smiled broadly. It was a drawing in color pencils of Samson high in a tree holding a fire rose in his hand. Thisbe was a fabulous artist and the picture was outstanding.

"Thiz, this is amazing! Thank you."

Lastly Castilia handed him a finely wrapped rectangular box in red paper and an orange bow. "Happy Birthday," she said. Samson unwrapped the box and found a wind chime Castilia had fashioned from sea glass and shells she had found at the beach. The glass hung from fishing line that was attached to a small piece of oak. It was small and simple but made a calming tinkle of music in the breeze.

"Wow, Castilia, you made this?"

"Yep. It wasn't easy. I found a how to page on the internet. The knots were the hardest part." she answered with pride.

"Thanks, it's wonderful. Thanks to all of you. These are the best presents ever!"

Thisbe pulled out the cake at this point and lit the candles. They all sang 'Happy Birthday' and Samson blew the candles out like a champ. The cake was dry and the frosting was not quite right but it was the best birthday cake Samson had ever tasted. He felt great and was now inspired. He jumped to his feet and turned to address his siblings, who knew by the look in his face what he was going to say. Castilia and Thisbe stood up. Wylde, who was sitting on a low branch of the oak tree, jumped down.

"I think we should..." Samson began, but as Wylde hit the ground a familiar sound rang in the air "Thunk."

Samson looked at Wylde's feet. "...make a visit to the chamber," Samson finished with a smile.

CHAPTER 29

Combustion

They cleaned up the picnic, uncovered the chamber door and quickly descended. Once inside, Samson felt whole again. The chamber felt oddly comfortable and familiar. It seemed that the murals were brighter and fresher, particularly the fire mural; it was if it was shimmering. Everyone was giddy with excitement to see Samson aflame again. They gathered around the center pool in their respective quarters to watch Samson show his stuff.

Samson felt empowered and almost overwhelmed, like he needed to release. He balled his fists then opened them with a burning rose levitating just above his palms. Everyone cheered. Samson could feel pressure rising in himself, the flower now danced and quickly engulfed his hands. The emotion of the last week was flooding out and burning up. Samson was working hard to control himself, but the pressure continued to build, it was almost painful. He looked at his brother and sisters with worried eyes, they were still cheering and clapping in delight.

"Guys," Samson said in a strained voice. "I think you need to stand back."

"What?" Castilia said as everyone got suddenly quiet at the seriousness of Samson's voice.

"Get back!" Samson strained against himself to hold back a torrent of emotion and energy. "Run!"

Castilia, Thisbe and Wylde quickly backed away to the wall of the chamber staring at their brother with wide eyes. Samson strained against the pressure for as long as he could, the flames had reached his elbows. The fire felt so good on his skin. He finally let it go.

"Swoosh!"

An intense white light filled the chamber. Castilia, Thisbe and Wylde had to shade their eyes as the heat filled the room. Their eyes adjusted and they saw a swirling orange and white flame surrounding Samson who was now levitating a few feet above the pool in the center of the chamber. The area just around his body was glowing blue, like an aura. His arms were outstretched and a look a serene pleasure washed his face. He was in ecstasy. Castilia, Thisbe and Wylde slowly walked toward their burning brother.

"Dude!" Wylde shouted. "Your clothes burned off!" He started laughing. "You're completely naked!"

"Oh hush, you idiot." Castilia chided. "You can't see anything through the flames and that not even important. Look at him. This is amazing."

"It feels great!" Samson yelled.

"Do you know you are floating?" Thisbe asked.

"Huh?" Samson said now aware that his feet where not touching the ground. He temporarily flailed his arms and legs like he was going to fall until he managed to regain his balance. He steadied himself and giggled. "Cool!"

He began to experiment by moving his hands and feet. Small movements allowed him to move this way and that. The aerodynamics lesson he had at flight camp came in handy here. His feet acted like a rudder and his hands and arms like flaps on a plane wing. Slowly he began to move around the domed chamber. Pointing his toes made him go higher and faster. Moving them up slowed him down and acted as brakes. Moving his arms and legs allowed him to turn right and left.

"I can fly!" he yelled in delight as he swooped around the room. Castilia, Thisbe and Wylde stared in amazement and cheered as he began to master the art of flying.

After a while, Samson felt very comfortable moving about the chamber. He could get up some speed flying in a tight circle around the dome. He wanted more space to see what he could do.

"It's too cramped in here. I need to head outside." He said moving toward the oculus.

"Wait!" Castilia screamed. "Remember the last time you extinguished when you exited the chamber."

Samson swooped down in front of Castilia. "Right." He said. "OK I'll take it slow and stay close to the edge so I can grab onto something if it happens. Wylde, stay under the ladder and try and break my fall if something happens."

"Are you crazy?" Wylde answered. "You would crush me AND you're on fire! You're on your own, fly boy."

"OK, OK. You're right." Samson said as he floated up toward the door. He paused at the opening. The sky outside had turned dark. Ominous clouds hung low. He wouldn't have much time before it started raining. It was now or never. Slowly he moved up until his eyes rose past the ground, he positioned his hands over the edge of the entry to grab it in case gravity took over. He paused. Nothing happened. He inched out further and further until he was floating just above the opening.

"Ha ha!" he laughed in glee. It worked. He did it. He spun in delight and rose higher in the air.

Castilia, Thisbe and Wylde watched with trepidation as Samson moved through the oculus. When he made it through, they could see his bright figure through the hole and cheered as he was spinning.

"Be careful!" Castilia yelled but the words barely escaped her lips when they heard a gun shot and saw their brother fall out of the sky and out of view. They stood there frozen not knowing what to do. After a few moments, the blur of a dark figure flashed over the hole in the direction Samson fell.

"NO!" they all yelled in unison. They scrambled up the ladder not thinking of what might be waiting for them.

226

CHAPTER 30

Bears

Samson hit the ground hard. "What the hell just happened?" he thought. He felt like he got hit by a Mack truck. He tried to sit up and get his bearings.

"Owww!" He screamed as a sharp pain shot through his left shoulder. He saw a fiery hand pass his eyes to support his left side. He had almost forgotten he was still engulfed in flame and just moments ago was levitating above the chamber entrance. He could hear Castilia's screams echoing inside the subterranean dome. He was able to look around in the dark to see he had ignited brush, grass and a small tree in his fall. The fire illuminated the area. There was movement in the brush just below the knoll as four dark figures emerged out of the darkness. Samson managed to get to his knees in a defensive posture, the pain in his shoulder was almost unbearable. He stared out across the burgeoning fire toward the approaching figures. They seemed to grow exponentially with every passing second as the flames spread over the area, flickering shadows over the landscape. The figures seemed to Morph into the shape of four black bears.

Samson's mind reeled, "Four bears? Seriously? THE four bears? This can't be possible," he thought to himself as he knelt there stunned beyond believe. The story of the Hehatu that Professor Fitch told him was real. Samson rubbed his eyes to make sure he knew what he was seeing.

The bears stopped at the top of the knoll. They all stood to their full height, looking down at Samson seeming to contemplate their next move.

"Give us the Amulet and you will be unharmed," a voice shouted from amongst the bears.

If this scene was not surreal enough, the talking bear now made Samson wonder if he was dreaming. Samson was unsure what to do next, so he did nothing. He continued to stare incredulously up at the four bears trying to ignore the intense pain in his shoulder.

The four bears moved in unison toward Samson, as they neared the flames Samson could see the figures were not bears at all but men in elaborate costumes. They did, indeed, have what looked like real bear head headdresses and large fur cloaks. The light glinted on sharp metal claws that each held in their hands. As they moved closer, the shadows and light danced upon them, exposing human faces that were painted black in elaborate patterns that reminded Samson of the tattooed faces of native South Pacific islanders. The light flickered again upon the men and the patterns on their faces made them look more ferocious. While the initial sight of the four bears was stunning and curious, these men definitely made Samson very, very frightened.

They began to fan out as they approached, raising the claws in their hands defensively. They moved cautiously and formed a semi-circle around him. Samson still did not move but he could tell his flame was not as bright as it had been. His shoulder throbbed and he was having trouble breathing. He was getting weaker.

"Hehatu only wants the amulet," the one directly in front of Samson said in a low gravely voice. "Give it to us and we leave you in peace." There was a long silence as they stared each other down.

Samson licked his parched lips. "What do you want it for?" he asked breaking the silence.

"That is not your concern," the man yelled sternly, surprising Samson. His voice became almost maniacal.

Samson looked around calmly. He knew he was woefully outnumbered but he didn't have many options. He had a sudden resolve.

"Well," he began slowly and quietly. The men leaned forward to hear him. "I'm pretty sure giving you my amulet is a bad idea, so unless you have some oven mitts, I think we are done here," he said bravely.

The bear smiled, showed crooked yellow teeth, and laughed a long low creepy laugh that made Samson's skin crawl. That was definitely not what he was expecting. His brief bravado evaporated. "That can't be good," he thought.

The main bear dropped his claws and two others moved to his side. From inside his cloak he pulled two large white gloves that covered his arms to his elbows. To Samson they looked very much like fireproof gloves.

"Awww, man. Really?" Samson said in despair, as the bears advance upon him.

Samson was terrified and stared wide-eyed at his attackers, his mind racing as to what to do next. The middle man was reaching his gloved hands toward him. The two others winced from the heat and stayed back a step or two. Samson was tense and expecting the worst. He raised his hand to fend of his attacker and tried to push him away when a jet of fire shot forth like a flame thrower from his fingers and completely covered the man with the gloves.

"Cool," Samson said softly in delight. For the third time tonight Samson was flabbergasted and elated at the same time. He could feel the energy flowing out of his arm. He could feel himself pushing the flame through himself, much like you exhale a deep breath. It was exhilarating but incredibly fatiguing. The pain in his shoulder worsened and he knew he couldn't keep this up much longer. He finally collapsed to the ground, breathing heavily. Lightning flashed across the sky. He looked up to see the middle bear slapping the mitts on his legs and body trying to extinguish the flames that were burning him alive. He had thrown his flaming headdress and cloak to the ground which lay burning beside him. The other two bears were running away lit up like torches in the night. They disappeared into the trees.

"AHHHH!" the bear screamed after he had put out the fire on his body, "you little asshole!"

Samson was weak. He could feel his fire dimming on his body. As cool as throwing fire was, he would not be able to do that again. He could now see blood trickling down his arm. The bear was enraged and looked at Samson with venomous eyes.

Samson prayed for help, but couldn't imagine where he'd get any at this point. The bear approached again in a uncontrolled rage. He began punching and pawing at Samson. Grabbing furiously at the talisman around his neck. The bulky gloves made it hard for the bear to grasp the necklace.

Samson did his best to block the bear's attempts but fatigue was setting in. He raised his hand again and pushed through it as he had done before but only sparks flew and fizzled into the night.

"Is that all you have left boy?" the bear growled mockingly, slapped Samson's outstretched hand down, and then made a renewed effort to grasp the necklace.

Samson's flame must have still been very hot as the bear could not stand close for long. He backed away smiling ominously, waiting for the flames to die down. Lightning flashed again and Samson heard his sister screaming at the top of the knoll.

CHAPTER 31

Rescue

Castilia climbed out of the hole first and saw Samson's conflagration had ignited the forest floor where he fell. He was still ablaze, but was much dimmer. The flames were dark red now. Two silhouetted figures were upon him, one was massive and looked like a bear with giant claws that glinted in the light of the fire slashing at him, while the other was simply dressed in black, and seemed to be smoldering. The smoldering one was trying to grab at Samson with thick gloved hands. Samson's flames were the only thing keeping them at bay. He was on the ground trying to fend them off with one hand, weakly, as his flame began diminishing by the second.

"NO!" Castilia screamed again. Wylde and Thisbe emerged from the chamber door to see their brother being attacked.

Wylde picked up a rock and hurled it at the two attackers, hitting the bear guy square in the back. He turned and looked their direction. He shouted something up the hill and pointed back to the kids. They looked in the other direction and saw 3 more black figures appear out of the darkness approaching rapidly. All were dressed in black, outfitted with similar but different uniforms. All three had knee high black boots and black pants. The one in the center had a knee length black coat that was belted tightly around his waist. He had a bandolier around his shoulder and a necklace of bear claws around his neck. His face was painted black with white stripes running down his nose and across each eye. He wore a type of goggles that glowed green in the darkness, which made him look alien and terrifying. The three all had some sort of of headdress made of animal bones, horns, and feathers. The middle one looked like he had a bird skull and beak at the center with black feathers surrounding his face. He was carrying a rifle in his hand.

The men approached fast and forced the kids back up against the old oak. Fear was welling up inside them. They had nowhere to go. Thisbe burst into tears as rain started to fall. Castilia was more terrified than she had ever been in her life, but was defiant and resolved to put up a fight. She and Wylde picked up rocks as the men approached.

"Hehatu only wants the boy. Stay out of this and you'll be unharmed!" shouted the middle man with the rifle. His voice was a low growl, forceful and terrifying. His painted face was a rage with glowing green eyes.

Castilia, Thisbe and Wylde were all frozen in surprise. "Hehatu?" Castilia whispered putting the pieces together. This was insane. Could the legend be true? They heard a low scream down the hill.

Castilia looked back at Samson, his flame was almost out. His attackers were advancing. The rain was falling harder now. There was no time.

"Screw you, mister, and the Hehatu!" she screamed, and thunder boomed in the sky and lightening flashed nearby. With that distraction, she threw the rock she had in her hand and hit the middle man square in the face. That same moment Wylde kicked the closest man in the ankle, which caused him to fall into the other two. Thisbe pelted the men with rocks, and then uncharacteristically yelled something in anger that was drowned out by crack of thunder.

"Run!" Castilia shouted, as lightening flashed brightly almost on top of them and the boom of thunder was deafening. The three kids scattered in the confusion.

Castilia ran toward Samson and could see his flame finally die out. The Hehatu with the gloves reached down and pulled the medallion from Samsons's neck and raised it to the sky in victory.

"NO!" Castilia yelled again, the rain fell harder as she sprinted toward him. Thisbe emerged from the darkness with a look of extreme intensity on her face as she stared at the Hehatu. She pointed to the man and screamed, "that's not yours!" at the top of her lungs. Castilia continued to run toward Samson but was suddenly blown backwards off her feet as lightening stuck the Hehatu's outstretched hand. He screamed an unfathomable scream and then fell lifeless to the ground. The second man with the bear claws was thrown back several feet and lay dazed on the ground, rolling back and forth in pain.

The lightening split a nearby tree that was now burning brightly. The flames illuminated the area and Castilia could see the three Hehatu she had just left were running toward her. There was nothing she could do buty stare at them helpless, rain and mud splashing in her face. The one with the rifle pointed it in her direction. Castilia stood defiant.

Lightening flashed again and struck the old oak tree. A huge branch sheared off the mighty oak and fell on the pursuing Hehatu, hitting them hard and trapping them under the mass of leaves and branches. Castilia jumped backwards and rolled in the mud, just avoiding barely the heavy branches.

Castilia managed to get herself up and out of the branches and run to Samson. She could hear sirens in the distance. Hopefully they were coming this way. The fire had spread to other trees at this point but the heavy rain was keeping it from getting out of control. Samson was face down on the ground and not moving when she got to him. She pulled him over. His breathing was very shallow. He had a bullet wound in his left shoulder and it was bleeding profusely. She ripped her shirt and applied pressure to the wound like she had seen on TV. Samson moaned.

The sirens grew louder and Castilia looked around to see the Hehatu retreating back into the darkness, dragging the gloved one behind them. Wylde was at the top of the hill, viciously throwing rocks in their direction. Thisbe appeared out of the darkness and ran in Castilia's direction with the picnic blanket in her hand. Thisbe and Castilia managed to wrap Samson's wound with a bandana. They used the blanket to keep him warm.

"Go get help!" Castilia screamed to Wylde as he started toward them. He stopped, reversed direction and took off in a flash.

Wylde arrived moments later with Mom, Dad and several firemen.

CHAPTER 32

The Hero

"He's awake I think." said a voice. "Mom, he's awake." Samson felt someone's warm hand cover his own and squeeze lightly. He opened his eyes to see his mother's smiling but haggard face over his own.

"Welcome back, sweetie." She said as tears rolled down her cheeks. Castilia, Thisbe, Wylde and Dad were all crowding around his mother smiling brightly. Thisbe was crying again. Samson was confused. All he knew was that his mouth was extremely dry.

"Water." he said softly through parched lips. They put a straw to his mouth and he took a long drink. It was as if he hadn't drank for days.

"You gave us quite a scare there, champ." Dad said.

"What happened?" Samson asked wearily.

"A lot." Castilia said smiling. They were all smiling. It was wonderful to see his family.

They all started talking at once. Then they organized themselves and took turns filling in the story. First, they explained that Argus and Howard were well and had confirmed most of

Samson's story. Argus took full responsibility for the midnight outing and explained how Samson had left in protest. Howard remembered seeing Samson's face pull him out of the house. The arson inspection determined the explosion at the Mitchell house to be the result of Mrs. Mitchell leaving the gas stove on by accident as she had been drinking. Apparently things were not going well with her marriage, which was also the reason Mr. Mitchell was away. A coffee maker on a timer created enough of a spark to ignite the gas. It was an unfortunate accident. It was, however, very fortunate that Samson was there as he single-handedly saved everyone. He was cleared of all charges and actually given an apology by Sargent O'Malley. The local paper ran a story on his heroics.

"That's a relief." Samson said, smiling. He hurt all over.

"Um. Where am I and what happened to me?" He said coughing. "Ouch." A sharp pain shot through his body.

"You're in the hospital, dear." Mom explained. "You were shot in the shoulder. The doctor's patched you up, but you lost a lot of blood. We were worried."

Castilia filled in how they were out for Samson's birthday picnic when a storm rolled in. They were packing up the picnic when Samson was shot by a group of strange men dressed in black. Luckily the storm struck and scared the men away.

Samson smiled. He was pleased the relayed events seemed to leave out the bits of his combustion and flight.

"Fortunately, the bullet went right through your shoulder and the doctors had an easy time patching you up. You have a good many bruises and cuts, but you'll be fine. Unfortunately, we have no clue what the whole thing was about. The police have no leads. They think a hunter mistakenly shot you and then tried to cover it up. However, hunting season is months away. It doesn't make much sense." Dad said, frowning.

"That seems to be my life as of late." Samson opined.

Samson had a slew of visitors during his stay in the hospital: Argus, Howard, Captain McKain and Mrs. Goodwyn, as well as many of his school friends. Sargent O'Malley even stopped by to apologize in person. Samson seemed to be a bit of a celebrity after the story in the newspaper. The mayor visited and gave Samson a Westville Declaration of Bravery certificate. The local television news station came by for an interview. Samson was much better at this point and managed to take a shower and comb his hair before they came. They all watched Samson's fifteen minutes of fame that night in the hospital on the Evening News. It was probably only two minutes, not fifteen, but that was plenty of attention as far as Samson was concerned.

He was able to come home the very next day, but he was still mostly relegated to bed rest. His shoulder still hurt something awful.

"I guess I should thank you for saving my life." Samson said to Castilia, Thisbe and Wylde when their mother was out of the room one morning.

"What do you mean?" Castilia asked.

"I was fairly out of it. but I do know that if you had not done what you did when you did, they would have killed me." Samson said.

"But it was mostly the storm." Thisbe offered.

"I've had a lot of time to think about that too," Samson said thoughtfully. "There is no way that the storm just happened. The rain, the thunder, the lightening, all at that moment, in that exact place. It's highly improbable. The three of you had to of made that happen. It's just too much of a coincidence. Plus, you had just given me my hope back. That birthday party was the best one ever. Anyway, I love all of you. Thanks."

"I know we haven't talked about it but your medallion is gone." Castilia said after an awkward moment. "I saw the Hehatu take it off your neck."

"Yeah, but for some reason, I don't feel worried about it," Samson answered drifting off contented.

"Well, I am worried about the Hehatu." Wylde commented. "They know your secret. They know who we are. That can't be good."

"Well, at least we know who we are dealing with," Castilia said thoughtfully. "Now we just need to find out WHAT we are dealing with."

"Whatever it is, whoever it is, we'll face them together," Thisbe said and they gave each other a knowing grin.

"Group hug!" she said as she jumped on her siblings making Samson wince in pain. He never said a word as he hugged them all right back.

EPILOGUE

The last day of summer vacation found Samson well enough to attempt a trip outside. He really wanted to see the knoll after what happened. His arm was in a sling and the pain was much better. He could get around without much trouble now. He wouldn't make it to school for the first week but he was getting better quick. Castilia, Thisbe and Wylde helped him up and got him dressed. Its not easy getting dressed with a hole in your shoulder.

It was a perfect late summer day. The sun was out, the sky was blue, and a light breeze kept the air from being too stuffy. The knoll still showed signs of the havoc of that fateful night. Most of the knoll had burned even though the firemen got the flames under control fairly quickly. The ground was charred where Samson landed and was attacked. A good bit of the low brush was gone now, turned to ash. The giant branch from the old oak still lay wilting on the ground. Samson wandered about trying to make sense of what happened that day. The wind was blowing lightly stirring up dust and ash.

"Well, I'm not sure what we've gotten ourselves into, but it doesn't seem like its all going to be very pleasant." he said to them. They all nodded pensively surveying the area as if it were representative of what was in store for them.

"Although shooting fire has got to be pretty cool," Wylde said breaking the tension. The wind kicked up blowing ash into the air.

Samson wiped his eyes with his good arm squinting through the ash as the wind suddenly died down. At that moment, something glinted in the sun and caught Samson's eye. He walked over a few steps, slowly bent down, his shoulder aching, and picked up his medallion.

THE END

BOOK TWO

Water: An Account of the Fantastic Adventures of the Presleys of Fox Hollow Farm

Coming Soon